Toby and Curt kissed, whilst Washington eased Toby's jeans down and began to suck his cock.

Washington could give a blow-job like no-one else. His warm, damp tongue vibrated like a motor but with all the teasing delicacy of a butterfly's wing. His thick lips applied and released pressure with an appallingly accurate sense of the exact needs of each individual cock. The occasional hard touch of his teeth sent penile nerve-endings into a delirium of pleasure.

Toby was such a treat to make love to because his natural response was always so ecstatic. He moaned whilst Curt was kissing his lips, but when the other boy went down to his sensitive neck, he howled. And his eventual cumming was preceded by a wail that seemed to emerge from the very soul of the earth. His body quivered like an aspen leaf, stilled, and then shuddered into nervous spasms of orgasm. Again and again and again his body jerked violently and the cum shot into the back of Washington's throat, filled his mouth and spilled back down the length of Toby's penis.

Other titles from
PROWLER BOOKS:

Fiction:

Diary of a Hustler
• ISBN 0-9524647-64

Slaves
• ISBN 0-9524647-99

Young Cruisers
• ISBN 0-9524647-72

Hard
• ISBN 1-902644-01-8

The Young and the Hung
• ISBN 1-902644-07-7

Aroused
• ISBN 1-902644-08-5

Shipmates
• ISBN 1-902644-14-X

Feeling Frisky
• ISBN 1-902644-15-8

Virgin Sailors
• ISBN 1-902644-03-4

California Creamin'
• ISBN 1-90264404-2

Brad
• ISBN 1-90264409-3

Active Service
• ISBN 1-90264406-9

Campus Confessions
• ISBN 1-90264411-5

Summer Sweat
• ISBN 1-90264410-7

Going Down
• ISBN 1-90264412-3

Photographic:

Planet Boys
• ISBN 0-9524647-13

Kama Sutra of Gay Sex
• ISBN 0-9524647-05

Travel:

New York Scene Guide
• ISBN 1-90264400-X

Paris Scene Guide
• ISBN 1-90264402-6

PARADISE PALACE by Peter Slater

Copyright © 1999 PETER SLATER.
All rights reserved. Peter Slater has asserted his right to be
identified as the author of this work in accordance with the
Copyright, Designs and Patents Act 1988.

No part of this book may be reproduced, stored in retrieval
system, or transmitted in any form, by any means, including
mechanicals, electronic, photocopying, recording or otherwise, without prior written permission of the publishers.

First printed November 1999 by Millivres Ltd, part of MPG,
3 Broadbent Close, 20 Highgate High St, London N6 5GG
web-site: prowler.co.uk
Cover photography Bjorn Andersen © 1999 Prowler Press

• ISBN 1-902644-18-2

British Library Cataloguing in Publication Data.
A catalogue record for this book is available from the British
Library.

Printed in Finland by Werner Soderstrom Oy.

Paradise Palace
PETER SLATER

PROWLER BOOKS

Chapter One

The boys at the palace were all in a tizz. Never it seemed had there been such excitement. In a week's time, Wendell Banks, legendary director of such films as Pizza Boy - He Delivers, Baseball Nights, College Holiday and The Never-Ending Fuck, was due to pay a visit. And there was a rumour that he was talent-scouting for his next movie. Some even surmised that he actually might want to set his next movie at the Paradise Palace. Why not, for heaven's sake? - there could be few places so appealing to the average red-blooded man.

The Paradise Palace was situated in acres of well-watered grounds deep in the Arizona desert. Originally built for a lunatic railroad magnate in the middle of the last century, for a hundred and fifty years it had withstood drought, marauding Apaches and the Depression. Then, when its last owner, an ancient widow woman - who had, so it was rumoured, favoured Geronimo, and who had spent her last years trailing late at night through the narrow corridors and mysterious passages by candlelight - departed this mortal coil, it had appeared for auction in Tucson one Saturday morning. By chance, a certain Texan millionaire had been visiting the town that day and, purely on a whim, had bought the place.

Initially, he had intended using it merely as a country retreat; but, ever a businessman, he soon realised its potential as a discreet boy brothel. Instead of the usual in-out of most city brothels, here customers would be invited to stay a weekend, or longer. It would be a classy joint, offering such attractions as an Apache Night, Tribal Initiations, Desert Games and much else. The themed rooms would include: 'Wigwam Suite,' 'Nights in the Desert,' 'The Company of Savages,' 'War Paint' and 'Injun Boys.' There would also be a sauna, games room, restaurant, cafe, bar and multiplex cinema; and, outside, the grounds would incorporate swimming-pools, a woodland walk, picnic areas and miniature golf-course. And so it came to be. For this, of course, the punters parted with big dollars. In the five years that the palace had been open,

Peter Slater

Sam Greatorix (our millionaire) had increased his fortune several times over.

Toby stood on a veranda outside the palace wall and scanned the desert through binoculars. He was naked. It was usual for the boys to be nude or semi-nude when around the palace. Toby's skin was light brown, his hair was blond and eyes an icy blue. The youngest of the boys, it was plain that his face had yet to see a razor; but his cock was one of the cheekiest and at most times appeared to be in a state of semi-erection. His sexuality was at its peak and half a dozen orgasms each day was his absolute minimum - which was just as well because, within the boys' own individual limits, the guests were allowed any boy, any how and at any time.

'No sign, yet?' asked Curt, who was lying on the swing bench reading Crime and Punishment. Curt was as dark as Toby was fair and the contrast made them a popular feature of the evening cabarets, when Curt's vigorous fucking would reduce Toby to whimpering ecstasy.

It was still only early morning, but Jed Howitzer - Wendell's usual leading man and producer - had announced that he would be travelling overnight from Tucson. A romantic, he had said that he was looking forward to driving beneath the desert moon. All the guests and the other boys were still asleep and the silence was profound.

Curt got off the seat and stood behind Toby. Toby felt Curt's long cock pressing against his thigh and he murmured appreciation. He murmured some more and threw his head back when Curt pinched a nipple and lightly bit Toby's neck, which might have been designed for vampires: it was highly erogenous, and, if anybody bit him there, Toby's reaction was instant surrender. Taking Toby's surging cock between thumb and two fingers, Curt began to masturbate him. Toby's body quivered with an intensity of pleasure such as only an adolescent can truly feel. The boys turned to face each other and kissed, lips against lips, tongues intertwined, for the longest time. Their pulsing cocks rubbed against each other and against their taut stomachs.

Paradise Palace

Toby began to feel Curt's strong, assured fingers massaging his buttocks and then slipping in to the welcoming crack. Toby writhed in welcome. Then came a new sensation. A warm, delicious moistness that at first touched only the periphery of his asshole and then gradually worked deeper. It was a tongue, taut and rigid - such a tongue, in fact, that to be rimmed by it almost felt like a shallow fuck. The tongue ranged high on Toby's male cunt and deep and low. It licked the back of his balls, the sensitive insides of his thighs. Finally, after one last penetration of his crack, it trailed wetly up Toby's spine.

Toby knew what to expect. He murmured 'Fuck me!' into Curt's mouth and, at the same time, felt the first firm hard thrust of the stranger's rubber-clad cock.

Curt pulled away slightly, holding Toby by the shoulders as the intensity of the fucking increased. Toby leaned towards his friend, his face desperate with longing, tongue searching for tongue; but Curt abruptly thrust him away and against the railings. Now the stranger - a built black stud by the name of Washington - established a steady rhythm, and Toby's breathing came in gasps. Curt went down the steps and took Toby's cock in his mouth through the railings. Whilst Curt masturbated, Toby was being fucked and fellated.

Curt was the first to come, shooting great wads onto the dust. Then the stud pulled out, and, peeling the condom from his cock, swung Toby round and down and came heavily in his face. Finally after a little help from Washington's hand and tongue, Toby came also.

A quickie to start the day. The three boys curled up around each other like cats on the porch and snatched a little more well-earned sleep. Pale brown, dark and pitch black, their contrasted colours were attractive.

In the distance, a small dark cloud like a smudge of pencil appeared, moving across the desert.

Toby felt a pressure against his cock. He stirred in his sleep and his pretty features were twisted by a small grimace, a shadow across the face of the moon. His lovely face settled once more into peaceful sleep

Peter Slater

until a further increase of pressure caused him to writhe with an increase of pleasure. His hips rose slightly off the ground. Although his cock was by now clearly awake, the rest of him slept on - not that this was that unusual. The sleeping boy smiled and his tongue licked his red lips.

It was Washington who awoke first. The sight that met his eyes caused a jag of lust to speed through his stomach and instantly stiffen his black cock. The purple head rose through the uncut foreskin and a crinkly vein began to pulse along the entire length.

There, standing over the boys, was Jed Howitzer. The man was tall, with crew-cut hair and a face that somehow possessed qualities both rugged and vulnerable. His broad shoulders and worked-out chest strained against a white linen tee-shirt that reached to just above his navel. A temptation-trail of fine hair led down to tight jeans that pressed hard against a clearly defined cock that might have been mistaken for a cosh. On Jed's feet were cowboy boots with spurs, and it was with one of these boots that he was teasing Toby's young cock.

Washington, overawed, could only gaze. The only part of him that moved was his gently pulsing penis. As he watched, Jed pulled a foil-wrapped condom from his pocket and tossed it to the ground beside the still slumbering Toby.

Curt awoke next. His natural reaction was to reach for Washington's penis and give it some slow relief.

A flicker beneath Toby's eyelids indicated that he was also soon to surface into blissful consciousness. The delicate eyelashes blinked, and then parted to release the famous powerful blue gaze. Barely a moment passed before that slim, lithe body curled gracefully up and towards the object of its gaze. Toby knelt before Jed and kissed the man's stomach before going on to nuzzle the front of his jeans. He moistened Jed's crotch with desperate tongue, and snaked the zip slowly down over rock hardness. The stiff cock needed only the parting of denim for it to flip out, erect, straight and true. Its size seemed even more than the incredible nine inches proclaimed on all Jed's publicity. If Toby was daunted, he did not show it. He took the penis sideways on, nibbling and licking as you might a giant hot dog. His mouth knew just the right amount of pressure to apply, a sensitive balance between pain and pleasure. Jed's trousers slipped below his knees and Toby's slim boyish hand played with his balls which hung huge and low, like those of a bull. He was a bull being favoured by a young colt.

Toby's lips and tongue found the glans of Jed's penis. Being uncircumcised, Jed's glans was normally sheathed and was, therefore, especially sensitive. It was the bull's weak point. Anyone - anyone - who licked or caressed this part of him would have the stud utterly within his power. The Master become the Slave.

Curt and Washington broke off their own lovemaking to look in astonishment as the great man, his eyes closed and face squeezed in ecstasy, began to whimper like a puppy. The temptation was too great, and they went over to assist their friend. Fulfilling a dream of a lifetime, Washington divested the man of his tee-shirt and kissed his lips. Curt stooped to retrieve the condom that Jed had dropped earlier. He tore the foil wrapper with his teeth and swiftly rolled the slick rubber onto his pulsing erection. Barely missing a beat, he dared to stroke his cock between Jed's buttocks.

Time seemed to stand still, the world lulled by gentle rocking and pulsing, until, tormented into instinctual action, Curt's cock took on a life of its own and suddenly plunged deep into the man's arse. Jed staggered forwards and bent at an angle. Washington and Toby fell away and then it was only Curt, the dark boy, and Jed, the man, fucking fiercely. The boy was possessed by a demon, it seemed, so hard and fast did he fuck. Jed fell to his knees, but never did Curt lose the rhythm. His body became saturated in sweat, you could hear the sound of his wet body slapping against the man's. All this time, he was silent. But then he began to groan as an orgasm built slowly, inexorably, deep within him. His groans increased as the minutes passed. The tension was building and building, but refusing to break.

'I can't come!' Curt almost sobbed, his lovely tortured face beaded in sweat.

Toby and Washington knew what to do. They approached on

either side and began masturbating close against him. They had no problems in climaxing. Their spunk spattered over Curt's face. The sight and scent was all that Curt needed. He exploded in a great howl of joy, a wave dashing against a rock. There were at least half a dozen spasms.

Curt slid away from Jed and collapsed onto the floor.

Jed grabbed Toby, his first love, and slammed the boy's face against his cock. Holding Toby by his hair, Jed viciously pumped the open mouth up and down the length of his cock. Toby gagged and could scarcely breathe. The cock plunged deep into the boy's throat and Curt and Washington began to fear for Toby's life. When they tried to pull him away, however, Toby stoutly resisted.

Eventually, Jed released the boy and pulled his cock away. With a quick couple of flicks of his wrist he came. The resulting torrent put them all to shame. The cum simply flooded from his cock. Most fell on Toby, but the other two were not slow to claim their share.

So we leave them for now, smearing cum upon one another's naked bodies, kissing, stroking and licking. Happy boys in Arizona.

Paradise Palace

Chapter Two

'My boys have got to be paid the top rates,' insisted Sam Greatorix. He blew out a great gust of cigar smoke.

Sam Greatorix was a plump man of sixty-three, grey haired and heavily jowled. Usually, as now, he wore a blue silk kimono patterned with dragons and forests. On his back a large silver moon rose behind pine trees.

They - Sam Greatorix and Jed Howitzer - were sitting on armchairs in Sam's office. Whilst Toby bathed the boss's feet in warm scented water, Curt knelt beside the chair and manicured his fingernails.

Sam's office contained a desk, leather armchairs and several large pot-plants. The wall behind Sam's desk was stuck with leather straps and chains. Two other walls were hung with pictures of boys of the world in various positions of copulation. One side of the room was taken up by a vast tinted window. Outside the window you could see the swimming pool, where, at this moment, a number of boys were playing with their clients. If you chose to look, you might see Herr Liebermann, the overweight German banker, who was swimming whilst being nibbled by half a dozen boys ('My little minnows,' he called them). But that's by the by.

'My boys have all been personally chosen, hand-picked by me,' Sam said. 'They're the best boys in the state - no, in all America - and I won't see them ill-used or underpaid. I want personal control of the script and full rights to change anything and to be present at each and every shoot. If there's anything my boys don't want to do, that must be respected. I won't have coercion.'

'That's no problem,' said Jed. He slid lower in his chair and adjusted his crotch comfortably with the palm of his hand. His heavy death's head ring sent a splinter of morning sunlight onto the opposite wall.

'I'm not asking for your comments, I'm merely giving you

statements of fact. And your director is Wendell B...'

'Wendell Banks. He did Boy Friday and Spurting...'

'I know the guy,' Sam interrupted. Something about Jed had clearly irritated him. 'Why hasn't he contacted me personally?'

'He thought you might prefer to hear the proposal from me first,' said Jed. 'I'm not just a star, I'm a producer and talent scout as well. I have to try out all my co-stars. Naturally I have to be first on any scene.' Again, he stroked his crotch, clearly implying that sexual favours would be given in exchange for a successful completion of the deal.

Sam was not slow to pick up on this.

'I don't want anything to do with your cock,' he said, bluntly. 'You're way too old for my tastes. Way too old.'

If Jed, at twenty-five, was at all miffed by this statement - potentially chilling for a porn star - he did not show it.

'What's Wendell offering - aside from your ageing body?'

Toby became more intent on Sam's left big toe in order to hide a giggle.

'Fifty thousand, cash.'

'And top dollars to the boys.'

'The boys get paid separately.'

'Top dollar.'

'Top dollar.'

Sam sighed. There was a long silence. Finally, he said, 'Ya know, Jed, you were good, real good in Pizza Boy. What happened?'

'I still get plenty work. More now than I did back then.'

'I tell ya what happened. Ya grew old. One moment you're a teenager, the world on its knees before you, the next... an old man.' Before Jed could protest, Sam said, 'In Ancient Greece you'd be an old man. Curt, sweetie...'

The dark-haired teenager, his eyes fluid and black, looked up. Sam trailed his fingers across Curt's mouth. The boy stood up and Sam began idly to masturbate him.

'Curt, read me a sonnet. There's the volume on the shelf there.'

Curt obediently went to fetch the book. Jed stared after him. The

Paradise Palace

kid had such a beautiful, pert little ass.

The boy returned with the book. His cock was half erect: he looked so sweet and sensual that the hardest bull dyke would surely have found him desirable at that moment. He stood before Sam and brushed a fall of dark hair from his face.

'Read us sonnet fifty-seven. And Toby, give him some help while he's at it.'

So Curt read and, whilst he read, Toby sucked his cock.

'"Being your slave, what should I do but tend
Upon the hours and times of your desire?"'

Curt paused and swallowed. His voice was gentle and moist. The sound itself was like a teasing tongue playing on cock and balls.

'"I have no precious time at all to spend,
Nor services to do till you require.
Nor dare I chide the world-without-end hour
Whilst I, my sovereign, watch the clock for you,
Nor think the bitterness of absence sour,
When you have bid your servant once adieu;
Nor dare I question with my jealous thought
Where you may be, or your affairs suppose,
But, like a sad slave stay and think of nought,
Save, where you are how happy you make those:
So true a fool is love, that in your will
(Though you do anything) he thinks no ill."'

Curt finished, his voice quavering over the final words as he was overcome by sexual passion. He put the book aside and he and Toby lay on the thick-pile carpeted floor and made love.

'Are you beginning to see where I'm coming from?' Sam asked Jed.

Jed, however, was clearly more interested in where the two boys were coming from. He had lowered his trousers zip and his fingers were stroking inside.

'I'd appreciate your full attention,' said Sam.

Jed accordingly, but reluctantly, restored respectability.

'What I'm after,' said Sam, 'is a class act. The world's had its fill of cheap porno movies. Boys fucking on sofas, sucking on beaches and banging away in fields… it's all been done a million times before. Boys with boys, boys with men, boys with sheep and Alsatian goddamn dogs. Dry boys, boys smeared with cream and oil, boys covered in chocolate, boys covered in egg and flour and cum. . . Uniforms, sports gear, chains… It's all passé. I run the classiest brothel in the world and so, if I'm to allow a film to be made here, I want it to be the classiest film.'

'I've already said that you'll be free to review the script.' Now it was Jed's turn to sound a little impatient. The sight of Curt's tight writhing buttocks was proving almost too much to bear.

'That's not enough. That was Shakespeare my little Curt read just now. Ever heard of the guy?'

'Sure!' protested Jed - although the name was one he always associated with a memory of being in a theatre and harangued from the stage by an old bearded man in a dress.

'I knew you guys were coming and it set me thinking, ya see. If ya do do a movie here, I want it ta be Shakespeare!'

Jed made a face.

'Don't worry!' said Sam. 'I'll rewrite the script as necessary. There's one play, ya see, I've got my eye on. What ya gotta bear in mind is that in Shakespeare's time all the actors were men - there was never a woman in sight. And he gave half the men women's names - which proves that Shakespeare was gay and that everything he wrote was gay. I tell ya, his whole oeuvre is a gay paradise. Anyway, this particular play is about a man and a boy marooned on a magic island where they're waited on by a fairy boy slave. What happens is that the old man's a magician and he causes a ship to be wrecked on the island so that all the sailors get to come ashore - then, basically, it's a sex free-for-all until the show's over. It's a great piece. I've seen it on the London stage, but of course the Brits edit out most of the original script. I wanna restore the true Elizabethan original - although of course as I

Paradise Palace

haven't got access to the goddamn British Museum it'll have ta be my interpretation of what the true original is. Nevertheless, it'll be closer than anything they produce at the Royal Shakespeare Goddamn Company. What ya reckon, Jed?'

'I'll have to ask Wendell.'

'No, you won't,' said Sam. 'If a movie gets made here, that's the movie that gets made. That or nothing. And don't think I care a damn about that fifty thousand dollars - if I want fifty thousand dollars, I get on the phone to the Taiwanese foreign minister and it'll be in my bank account tomorrow. And if I want a hundred thou' - why, I'll just give the Houses of Parliament in London a ring. There's one or two government ministers who'll happily pay any amount to preserve a certain silence around certain events in their past. If you were thinking I was gonna allow a few lights and a hand-held video camera operation at the Paradise Palace, you were sadly mistaken.'

A red light began to blink from a bank of lights above the door. 'Curt, Toby! Mr Sikorski needs some attention in the Rio Grande. Go to it!'

At first, so bound up were they in passion, that the boys took no notice. And when Sam attempted forcibly to separate them they turned their sexual attentions onto him. He had to be firm and slap them to order. Eventually, hand in hand, with cocks high, they went to perform their duties.

'So?' asked Sam, when the boys were gone.

'I think we can do business,' said Jed.

'I know it. Now get over here and give me some head.'

'Thought I was too old for you?'

'It's a Thursday, ain't it? If a man can't bend the rules on a goddamn Thursday when can he?'

Chapter Three

'Boys!' Sam Greatorix entered through the double doors of the gym hall and called for attention through a megaphone. He was flanked by Curt and Toby. Behind them came Jed Howitzer.

The hall was filled with naked boys working through their regular pre-prandial gymnastics session. Boys were bouncing on a trampoline, climbing wall bars, vaulting over horses, lifting weights and performing graceful acrobatics on floor mats. This was among the most popular features of the Paradise daily timetable, and every boy at the palace was required to attend.

'Boys!' Sam called again. 'And honoured guests,' he deferred, with a small bow, to the gentlemen who were working-out at the same time. 'I'd be grateful for your attention.'

The creaking and thumping of a gym full of exercising boys gradually gave way to a silence leavened only with the heavy breathing of young, sweating bodies.

Sam and his entourage climbed onto a stage at one end of the gym. Sam was in his customary gown, the boys were naked, Jed wore jeans and sweatshirt. When Jed had suggested that he, too, should go naked about the palace, Sam had protested, 'Pur-lease! You'll frighten the horses!'

'Boys! I'd like to introduce you all to a fella who's gonna be with us for a while. You may not recognise him with his clothes on, but this here is J-e-edd Howw-wit-ZERRRR!' He thundered out the name.

Jed's smile could not hide his uneasiness. Sam's hot and cold attitude towards him was bewildering and unsettling.

The boys whooped and clapped a hero's welcome.

'Jed's come to make a film and…'

Another tumultuous round of applause interrupted him.

'… And he's looking for some co-stars here!'

At that, there came yells and whistles, clapping and stamping of bare feet.

Paradise Palace

'Lookee here, Jed!' and 'Me! Me!' came from boys thrusting themselves forward and proffering their cocks. 'I'm the one! You saw me the first! Me! I go on forever!'

'Okay, okay! Simmer down, now', Sam shouted. 'I wanna tell ya how the casting's gonna be done. It won't be easy. I know that each and every one of you would be good in a porno movie - you're all beautiful and hung, that's how come you're here in the first place. But this movie will be different and I'm gonna cast the main parts strickly on an intellectual basis.'

The boys were eerily quiet. Some even stopped breathing.

'This movie,' Sam continued, 'will be Shakespeare. A play of his called The Tempest. Hands up who's heard of it.'

All hands went up, but this was probably more to do with the fact that the boys had been conditioned to automatic response whenever Sam called out 'Hands up!' rather than with any great knowledge of English literature.

'I don't believe you,' Sam said. 'But that's by-the-by. You may not have heard of it, now, but believe me you'll know it inside out through the next few weeks. I've just been on the phone to the Arden Shakespeare Company in Oxford, England, and they're gonna rush me two dozen copies of this here play.'

That he could have got the scripts a great deal more cheaply in America did not interest him - they would be that much more authentic if mailed from England. The simple, romantic part of his nature imagined the Arden publishing company to be situated in a timbered Tudor house deep in an oak forest.

'Once the copies come, you'll each get one and I'll ask you to go away and study it. Then when you've got the gist of the story, we'll hold the auditions. The best parts will go to those boys who can impart most meaning to the poetry. Alright. That's enough of all that. Time now, I think, for a little community singing. Pull that piano out, boys!'

A group of eager helpers ran to the piano and pulled it out from a corner. Sam Greatorix got down from the stage, sat at the piano, lit his cigar and began to play 'God Bless America'! On cue, an American flag

Peter Slater

unfurled above the stage and, from the ceiling, a thousand red, white and blue fairy lights began twinkling. Boys and men sang away lustily. Next came 'Yankee Doodle', 'Listen to the Mockingbird' and 'De Camptown Races'. Community singing was a popular event at the Paradise Palace. All the boys were required to learn the words to standard songs and there was usually a good turn out of guests for the occasions - although whether that was to do with love of music or delight in sucking a boy's cock whilst he sang 'Yankee Doodle', was perhaps a matter for debate.

Wendell Banks arrived a week later, on the same day as the boxes of Tempests. The most famous gay porno film director in America was not without clear defining characteristics.

A welcoming party of boys rolled out the red carpet to where his cream cadillac stopped outside the main gate of the palace, and out stepped a black dwarf dressed in a glittering gold suit, with gold shoes and gold wide-brimmed hat to match. He wore dark glasses and was smoking a cigar.

'Wendell Banks!' Sam welcomed the guest. Sam himself was wearing tuxedo and tie. The men, in contrast to the naked boys who were lined up on either side of the red carpet, seemed hugely over-dressed. 'We're honoured to have you here! Deeply honoured!' Sam flinched on the adverb as Wendell grasped him by the balls.

Wendell made his way up the line of boys, inspecting them as was appropriate for a guard of honour. He made a point of shaking each boy by the cock, and some of them received more than a mere shake - his face was just the right height - so that, by the time he had finished he left behind him a trail of salutes.

'Don't think I'm small,' was the first thing Wendell said when Sam showed him his suite of rooms. 'Built like a pony, hung like a horse!'

'Never doubted it, Mr Banks.'

'Call me Wendell. Do ya wanna watch me shower so I can prove it to you? I'll be frank, Sam, and say right out that you're the kind of man I like to get my cock into. Believe me, I've seen so many boys I'm sick

Paradise Palace

of the sight. Give me maturity any day. I like a body that's been lived in a while. And yours certainly looks lived-in - ya must have paid off the mortgage several times over by now, hey? Hey? Ha, ha, ha!'

The rooms - or, rather, one vast room in three sections - were luxurious. Richly-curtained, carpeted and furnished. The bed was a four-poster, the walls and ceilings mirrored. Wendell, however, was not impressed. He described the set-up as "Sixties-brothel". 'But never mind, Sam, I'm happy anywhere so long as I've got company. Hey?' Again, he grabbed Sam's balls.

The boys, who had carried in Wendell's trunk and his vast number of cases, hid their smiles.

'Company?' said Sam. 'That's what this place has got loads of!' A swing of his arm indicated not just the present boys but was clearly meant to include the whole troupe.

'Surely,' concurred Wendell. 'But how many are over forty? And how many can talk to me about Shakespeare and Wagner - that's what really turns me on, and my boy, Jed, has been telling me all about your little plans so I know you just ain't any old air-head. Where is that Jed, anyways?'

'There's a dying Texan oil man fallen in love with him, so he's a bit taken-up at the moment. We've got a solicitor flying in by helicopter, should there be any question of changing a Will.'

'That's ma boy!'

'So Jed has been talking to you?'

'I know your plans.'

'And?'

'I concur entirely! My God, of course I do! This is the kind of movie I've waited all my life to make. The Tempest! My God! It would be the crowning achievement of my career. What's the angle?'

'We cut out all the Victorian additions and restore the original gay text. It's a Gay Classic - a fact which most people seem to have forgotten.'

'My feelings exactly! - Sammie, we are uncannily on the same wavelength, here. In fact, I'm so enthusiastic about this project I want,

Peter Slater

for the first time in my career, to be an actor/director. I want to be in this thing. I've wanted all my life to play the part of Prospero, ya know that?'

Sam said nothing as his own greatest hope was dashed against the rocks.

'Now Prospero,' Wendell continued, 'the ageing stud who lives on the island with his toy boy and a fairy, is constantly subjected to gay-bashing and homophobic abuse from one Caliban, a monster. In my opinion, Caliban is the greatest part that Shakespeare ever wrote - Marlon Brando would be great in it. So why don't you take it on? It'd be a challenge, but I can sense you'd be up to it.'

'I'll think about it,' said Sam. 'But hey, look, you've just travelled three hundred miles across the desert, we can't go straight into discussing business. Don't you wanna take a shower and rest up for a while?'

'Sammie, I didn't become the greatest director in the world by washing and sleeping in all my spare moments. Keep moving all the time, that's my motto. Let the world sleep - Wendell Banks is too busy. Ya know how much money I made with my broker on the phone whilst I was on my way here today? Fifty thousand dollars! - we're investing in a new dildo venture. Hey, okay, I can afford a break! Fuck me, Sam!'

Sam took a step backwards. 'Sorry, Wendell, I'm just not up to it right now.'

'In the shower. I gotta take a shower and I can kill two birds with one stone.'

'Take a boy.'

'I told ya, I'm sick ta death of boys! I need you.'

'Another time, eh?'

'You the only man around here?'

'Fraid so. Except for our House doctor, Doctor Max; but he's taken the hypocritical oath and has sworn himself to celibacy.'

'That's bad news. Baad. But I can wait. I'll have you in the end, Sam, mark my words! You just mark by words!'

Sam made a hasty retreat from Wendell's room, telling him that when he had freshened up he should come to his office and they could

– 16 –

discuss the project.

'Ring the bell,' Sam said, indicating a long, thick tasselled bell-pull by the door, 'and a boy'll come and escort you. Or, if you prefer, there's an intercom by your bed. With that you can summon anything you like at whatever time you like. Chocolate chip ice-cream and a little fellatio at three in the morning? - no problem! Steam towels and a Roman orgy before breakfast? - you got it! I'll see ya later!'

'Alligator!' Wendell raised a hand.

Outside the door, Sam whispered to the boys who had followed him out, 'Look, get back in there and give him some relief - the guy's obviously suffering from sexual dementia. Rape him if you have to.'

The boys duly returned. Two naked, blond-haired, blue-eyed nineteen-year-olds with smooth skin and drop dead smiles - who could have resisted them?

Wendell Banks.

'Get the fuck outa here!' he shouted. 'A guy doesn't want two overgrown Barbie dolls ta get in the way when he's taking a shower!'

Peter Slater

Chapter Four

Toby, Curt and their friend Washington - the tall black boy from the Bronx - were walking in the Paradise Garden. This was a walled-off enclosure, an acre in size, open only to the boys. It was their own space and here they went to relax and recuperate and simply to get away by themselves for a while. Sprinklers played constantly over lawns, there were walks shaded by mimosa and vines, thick shrubbery and flowering trees. Peacocks slipped in and out of the shadows.

The boys were dressed in jeans and tee-shirts and each held a copy of The Tempest. They had been instructed to read it and, if they liked, to choose parts for themselves (Caliban and Prospero excepted).

They came to a mossy bank by the side of a water-lily covered pond. Here they sat and made themselves comfortable. A dragonfly hovered low over the water; and, feeding at a nearby hibiscus, a hummingbird hovered graceful as a happy thought.

After a time of quiet reading, Toby said,

'Man! What's all this about? Make any sense to you?'

'Nope,' said Washington.

'The guy ain't English,' said Curt.

'Course he's English!' said Toby. 'But he's dead English. This was how they all used to speak.'

'Then how the hell did they get along? How did they understand each other?' asked Washington.

'They didn't,' said Curt. 'That's why they're dead.'

'At least it's clearly gay, though,' observed Toby.

'Oh, sure!' said the others, sounding confident, although they weren't in the least.

'I mean, all these sailors, and that,' Toby continued. 'Couldn't be anything else. Did I ever tell you about when I was a cabin boy on a sailing ship crossing the Pacific?'

'Only about a hundred times,' said Curt.

'That was a dream orgy,' continued Toby, ignoring him. 'Thirty

Paradise Palace

sailors, all gay as fuck and not one of 'em over twenty five. It was a wonder we didn't ever get shipwrecked, considering the lack of attention we gave to steering the boat. We found some dream islands, too…'

'Look,' interrupted Curt, 'Much as we'd like to hear about your life as beat-off fantasy, we've got to read this goddamn play.'

'Okay, okay! Sorry I ever drew breath! Let's get back to master Shakespeare… "Where should this music be? In the air or the earth? It sounds no more, and sure, it waits upon some god of the island…" That's this Ferdinand, right? Now, he's a sailor who's been wrecked on this island where Miranda (who's really a boy) and Prospero (who pretends to be his father but is really his lover) are living. Now I bet you what you like that this Ferdinand will fall in love with this Miranda, so I bags the part of Miranda.'

'And I'll be Ferdinand, then,' said Curt.

'Hey, really? That's sweet.'

They leant against each other and kissed.

'So where's that leave me?' protested Washington, stroking the inside of Toby's thigh and gliding his hand upwards.

'Read on and see!' Toby suggested, breaking away briefly before once again meeting Curt's tongue with his own.

Toby and Curt kissed, whilst Washington eased Toby's jeans down and began to suck his cock. Washington could give a blow-job like no-one else. His warm, damp tongue vibrated like a motor but with all the teasing delicacy of a butterfly's wing. His thick lips applied and released pressure with an appallingly accurate sense of the exact needs of each individual cock. The occasional hard touch of his teeth sent penile nerve-endings into a delirium of pleasure.

Toby was such a treat to make love to because his natural response was always so ecstatic. He moaned whilst Curt was kissing his lips, but when the other boy went down to his sensitive neck, he howled. And his eventual cumming was preceded by a wail that seemed to emerge from the very soul of the earth. His body quivered like an aspen leaf, stilled, and then shuddered into nervous spasms of orgasm. Again and again and again his body jerked violently and the cum shot into the back of Washington's throat, filled his mouth and spilled back down the length of Toby's penis.

It took the boys the best part of their rest day to finish reading the play. There were so many interruptions - not least from Swing and Swung, the twins, so named because Swing's cock swung to the left and Swung's cock swung to the right. The twins had green eyes and shoulder-length black hair and, because of their smouldering Native-American features, looked best dressed in loin cloths and sporting war paint. Riding ponies they were an absolute wow, the vigour of the animals seeming to impart some extra touch of wildness and sexual possibility to their lithe bodies.

Advancing in Indian garb, their smooth brown chests smeared with recent cum, they were a distraction to the three boys by the lake. The reading had progressed as far as Act Two scene Four; but scene Five would have to wait.

'Whose cum?' asked Washington, as the boys walked up.

'His!' they said as one, pointing to each other.

'Oh, God, that really turns me on!' said Washington, with an apologetic air and, Swung's loin cloth being in just about the right position, he leant forward and nuzzled the huge bulge. The cock flipped easily out and up.

And that was that for the next half hour.

But to their credit, the boys eventually did finish the play. In the end, they each took on a part and read aloud, stopping every now and again for much needed explanations and workings-out ('What the fuck's going on now?' was an oft-repeated cry.) Perhaps the achievement of the endeavour was not so much to do with love of literature or intellectual dedication as with the fact that none of the boys ever disobeyed Sam in anything. What Sam said, went. He it was who had to be obeyed. This obeisance Sam obtained a) through his natural magnetism, b) because the boys genuinely liked him and wanted to please, and c) because the boys enjoyed their work, were extremely well-paid and did not want to run the risk of losing a lucrative career. Those boys who stuck it with Sam for the average three-year term were financially secure for life - more than that, they were rich for life.

Evening was approaching as Washington embarked upon the last lines:

"'Now my charms are all oerthrown
And what strength I have's mine own
Which is most faint…'"

Chapter Five

Sam and Wendell spent the day in Sam's office, hammering out a viable screenplay from the ancient text.

Their inescapable conclusion was that the Victorians had added an awful lot of guff to Shakespeare's original play and, as well as much cutting, there were a lot of extra scenes that needed to be added in order to restore the spirit, at least, of the gay original.

The true story, they concluded, ran something along these lines: Prospero, gay Duke of Milan, was living in exile on an island with his boy lover Miranda, fairy boy slave Ariel and jealous butch-type Caliban. Fancying a bit of rough, Prospero - a magician - causes a storm to rise and shipwreck a boatload of sailors onto the island. Ferdinand, one of the sailors, falls in love with Miranda. Prospero says he can have the boy if he passes a series of tests. Cue scenes wherein Ferdinand's sexual ability is put to severe trial. Ferdinand wins through in the end and gets to fuck Miranda. The penultimate scene is a great banquet with ends with sailor boys, assorted magic sprites and fairies fucking each other amongst grapes, mangoes and falling petals. Prospero takes the boat and sails back to Italy with Ariel. Cue music (Wagner's Transformation Music from Parsifal).

'Queen Elizabeth should make you a knight, for services to literature,' said Wendell to Sam, when they had put the final full-stop in place. 'Now get yer dick out and show us what you're made of.'

'Wendell! What is it with you? I can offer you the finest studs in Arizona - what do you want with me, an ageing brothel madame?'

'Your mind, Sam. You never heard the saying that the brain is the greatest sex organ of them all?'

Despite himself, Sam was a little deflated by the comment. He had hoped to be told that, despite his years, he had an exceptionally youthful and fanciable body.

'Sure I've heard it!' Sam replied. 'I just never heard any cruising man quiz another on Sophocles before making out with him, is all.'

Paradise Palace

'You ain't never been cruised by me before,' said Wendell. 'But we can save it for later. When shall we begin casting?'

'Soon as you like!'

'Tonight?'

'After dinner will be fine. Now I'm going for a pedicure, right now. Care to join me?'

'Why, sure! My poor old toes could do with a bit of care and attention.'

Sam took Wendell on a circuitous route to the beauty parlour in order that his guest might be able to get some sort of feel for the palace. They walked across marbled halls where naked boys sat playing with some of the guests, through arched corridors, down wide staircases, across a courtyard where, in the centre, a fountain played into a pool vivid with goldfish and water lilies. In a small interior garden planted with a lawn, and with rose bushes, shrubs and fruit trees around the edges, a group of boys and men were painting each other.

'They're an Injun raiding party,' said Sam. 'They'll be riding out on ponies later, in search of the enemy camp.'

'What enemy?'

'Oh, that'll be a party that went out last night. They'll be camped out in the hills. When the raiding party find 'em all hell'll break loose. It's one of the most popular excursions at the palace. We're always oversubscribed. Some of the guests like to go as hunters, others like to be the hunted. It's great fun - imagine sitting camped by your fire not knowing if at any minute the most gorgeous tribe of Indians is going to jump out from behind the rocks and have their way with you. Not everybody's idea of a good time, but if you like the idea of being stripped, tied up and then buggered by a marauding Apache, then this is the one event you must sign up for.'

'I might just give it a miss this time around.'

'You're civilised, ain't ya?' said Sam.

'No,' said Wendell, 'I'm just one of them thar wild niggers in disguise - ya never read Faulkner and the times of Colonel Sutpen?'

'Sorry, I wasn't being ironic. No, I mean, well, you are civilised.'

'I like a glass of Italian wine and a touch of Dante, now and again.'
'So do I, Wendell, so do I.'
'I can tell it by the way you've laid out this place.'
'Sure.'
'So, come on, Sam, let's make it together!'
'Gee, Wendell, it's our minds that are matched, that's all.'
'When the marriage of true minds, Sam, baby, when the marriage…'

'It's a pleasure having someone of your intellectual calibre staying at the palace, it really is. But I've never had sex with anyone who was my intellectual equal - it's a recipe for disaster…'

'We'll see, Sammie, we'll see… Ya know I've got nine inches tucked away down there?'

'For Chrissake I don't care if you've got a fucking mortar cannon.'

'For an intellectual you can be pretty crude at times.'

'You started it.'

'This palace will be the perfect setting for the movie - a palace in the desert, it'll be a kind of metaphor for Prospero's island… This movie's gonna be my masterpiece.'

The beauty parlour was empty save for a man who looked uncannily like Al Gore, and who was sitting in an armchair, his feet resting on a stool while being tended by a boy.

As soon as they entered, another boy came up to them and said, 'What's it to be, sirs?' He was about twenty, long fair hair cascading about his naked shoulders. His slim body was totally shaved, and Sam ran his fingers across the smooth pubic area around his cock and balls.

'Aaron,' said Sam. 'This is Wendell Banks. He's here to direct a movie - and, incidentally, it just now strikes me that we could give you a vital part. But in the meantime, we're both in need of a pedicure. Ricky around?'

'Sure thing!' Ricky appeared as if from nowhere. Ricky was likewise shaved, but his razor had continued over his head so that every part of him was exceptionally smooth. He was rather gauche - either in reality or through affectation - and stood so close to Wendell Banks that

Paradise Palace

his large, circumcised cock pulsed against the man's cheek. Wendell took it in his mouth as a dog would a bone. You could tell he was not terrifically interested in fellatio, however; it was merely an act to ease the passing of time.

Sam sat in an armchair and Wendell clambered up into one beside him. The little man sat like an elf, with his legs straight out before him. The boys set to work.

'Ya know The Doll's House?' said Wendell, lighting a cigar.

'Play by Ibsen?'

'I love ya, fella! - yeah, that's the one. The Doll's House - that's what I call my house. Everything's in what ya might call miniature. Tiny chairs, tables - it's all at my level. The mirrors, clocks, paintings on the wall - everything. Except the bed. I need a big bed because I like big men. Big, old men. Grey hair, wise faces and bodies full of experience and skill. Ya can't teach experience - okay, most boys can do all sortsa clever things, but they won't have those little extra touches and skills that ya only get after a lifetime of fucking. When I have sex with a boy, it's only in the line of duty - if I've gotta teach him a new technique for a movie. When I sleep with a real man, that's pure pleasure. I'm surprised, quite honestly, that you don't feel the same way. Don't all these naked boys make you a little jaded?'

'Nope!' said Sam, taking a cigar himself from a box built into the arm of his chair. He noted that Wendell had not offered him the spare one that was in the top pocket of his jacket. 'Never. Living amongst pretty boys it's like everlasting springtime in New England. A man never tires of beauty.'

'But beauty is subjective.'

'If my boy, Toby, had his cock halfway up your ass you wouldn't say that.'

'If your boy, Toby, had his cock halfway up my ass I'd call the cops.'

'That's only your fantasy!'

'Touché, Turtle. Changing the subject - don't you think Aaron, here, would make a great Ariel? - the fairy boy spirit who's Prospero's

Peter Slater

slave.'

Aaron, who was tending Sam's feet, looked up with a pretty smile. His pure white teeth were especially adorable.

'Ordinarily he would. But I've got that part marked down for my boy, Toby. He'll be great in the part, I promise ya. He's got just about the neatest sweetest cock you'll ever see, and he can read poetry like a maestro. He's got a real feel for verse.'

'When are we gonna hold the auditions?'

'The boys've got their regular weekly clap clinic and safer sex lecture this afternoon, so we can't start till tomorrow. But there's no hurry, eh? And it gives 'em all a bit longer to finish reading the first script. I vote we photocopy our new edition and not give it out until the auditions. Let's see how the boys react when they come to it cold. Heh, heh!'

Sam laughed at his poor pun. Wendell, naturally, did not.

Paradise Palace

Chapter Six

Toby was lying naked on the double bed in his room. In one hand he held a portable phone, in his other, his cock.

He was on phone duty. Those boys who had the aptitude and special skills needed for this were required to fit in a specified number of hours each week. The work carried with it a good financial bonus, and if, as in Toby's case, the boy enjoyed it, then it was easy money. One might have thought that phone sex would not be a popular feature in a brothel when the real thing was so easily to be had. But not at all. Many clients only wanted sex by phone. They enjoyed the atmosphere of the palace and the presence of the boys, but they did not care for the messiness of the act itself. A good jerk off was what these men wanted. And it was what they got.

'Aaaah!' groaned Toby in a high pitch. He squirmed on his red silk sheets. 'Please, sir! Please! Harder, sir! Aaaaah! Fuck me deeper!'

His smooth chest was stained with the cum of earlier orgasms, and he was approaching his third. His hand gripped his rigid cock where a pearl of pre-cum was poised on the tip of the glans. Sweat beaded the boy's brow and his face ached with longing. Harder and harder, he pulled at his cock. He seemed out of all control.

'Please cum in me! Oh, please cum, sir! Fill me with your hot spunk! Aaaaaah! Aaaaaaah! AAAH! AAAH! AAAH! AAAH! AAAAAAAAAAAAAAAAAH!' Toby's cock spurted a flop of cum straight onto his face, then another high on his chest, and another and another. His groaning slowly subsided into short gasps of relief.

The groans and gasps were echoed down the phone as another customer registered his satisfaction.

Toby continued to sigh softly until, 'Okay, Mavis, you may go back to your mistress, now!' came the voice through the phone.

'Thank you, sir. Thank you.'

Toby clicked the instrument off and lay back exhausted. Needing a short break, he switched on call diversion (Carl, who was on duty at

Peter Slater

the same time, would have to field the next call) and reached for the book by his bed. It was a volume of Walt Whitman's poetry. But so whacked out was he that he had read no more than half a dozen lines before he fell spontaneously asleep. Bless him.

A quick catnap - ten minutes - was all he needed, however, to feel fully refreshed. He awoke, stretched and mewed (still a pussy!) and set the phone back on.

He was reading 'To a Western Boy' when the phone gently trilled.

'Hiii!' Toby answered, a slight crack in his voice as if from a virgin about to be deflowered.

'I want to be tied naked to a chain gang in a Mississippi swamp.'

'You got it!'

'And I want my masters to be cruel boys who whip and whip me.'

'We are.' Toby turned on the tape that played the sound of a crashing whip.

Thwackkk!

'Aaa!' came the man's voice.

'You better get back in line,' ordered Toby.

Thwackkk!

'You boys are wearing leather jackets, caps and thigh boots, but nothing else.'

'That's right,' said Toby.

'The heat and the flies are unbearable and we're covered in mud, but you don't give a shit.'

'Why should we?'

'You shouldn't. We're in that chain-gang 'cos we're bad men. We're muggers and murderers and all kindsa shit and we gotta serve our time...'

Having recognised the voice as belonging to a mild-mannered, sweet-natured priest from Wisconsin, Toby knew that all this was even more extreme fantasy than that which he usually heard. But it was fun.

'And ya know what the worst torture is?' the priest continued ' - seein' all you boys and your cute faces and cocks and asses and not bein' able to touch or nothin'.'

Paradise Palace

'You're makin' me hard,' said Toby. And it was true.

'That's right. All that hard young boy cock and we can't get to touch. But then ya know what happens?'

'Try me.'

'Ya make a mistake. Two of us break free and we run off into the swamp tied together but free of all the others. And then two of you boys chase after us - only you get lost pretty quick in all that mud and overhanging vines and stuff and we ambush you. We jump out at ya and tumble into the mud and we finally get our revenge on all that cock teasing, as we plunge our cocks into your tight quivering asses. We fuck 'em so hard you yell out. I wanna hear ya yell how it's gonna be...'

Toby wailed.

'Ya like it, don't ya?'

Yeah!' groaned the boy.

'In so fucking deep! the mud splashin' up all round us, the swamp birds flyin' around callin' out for their mates. Your smooth skin gettin' covered in mud, your hair caked in mud, all of yer mud, all yer innocence lost in the swamp water...'

'Yeahhh!'

'And then I cum! Ahhhhhhhh!'

The caller hung up abruptly. Short and sweet. Ah, well, Toby would save his orgasm for the next caller. Sometimes even boys need to regulate the number of their orgasms.

Toby took up the book again.
"We two boys forever clinging..."

Oh, that Walt Whitman knew it all! Sometimes Toby felt that he would like to live forever with another boy's cock permanently up his ass. The ideal would be to lie like frogs attached and up to their necks in warm water. Eventually they would sink under and drown in a state of unalloyed bliss.

The phone rang.

'Hello,' said Toby, injecting into his voice an extra-special ache.

'My fantasy is that I'd like to be fucked stoopid by a baseball team in a muddy stadium and I want to be watched by a crowd of fifty thousand naked men and boys who are all jerking off.'

'Yeah!' said Toby. He wet his palm and passed it over the tip of his penis, in order to intensify the sound of his wet wanking.

'The baseball team are fucking me and fucking... and the crowd are jerking off and there's just the sound of all these thousands of guys just getting off on the sight of me being gang-banged by the team.'

'I can buy into that,' said Toby.

'Fifty thousand men and boys all jerking off...'

'Fifty thousand.'

'Miles and miles of long, hard cock. And there's boys cumming already, only they're so potent they cum and just carry on jerking. It don't make no difference to them, they can have one climax after another: chain climaxes... And the air's filling with the scent of cum and the groans're growing louder and louder. One man cums inside me and another just takes over, climbs on top and thrusts himself in. I don't know who it is and I don't care, 'cos I love 'em all. I just know it's a good strong hard man all muscles and thick thighs and a heavy cock and balls. I can feel the balls slapping away on the back of my thighs. This man's a real bull, he bites my neck and snorts like he's a bull on heat. Take that, fucker, and that!'

Toby raised his buttocks off the bed and flipped his cock and balls around with his hand.

There was a long silence punctuated only by the sound of heavy breathing. Then the man said, 'And the crowd all build to a climax together. They know there's gonna be a moment when they all cum and I'm gonna cum with them at the same time they're gonna roar and I'm gonna roar It's building so slow and so fast all those boys just lusting after hard cock... Aaah, aah, aah... AAaaaaaaAAAAAAAAAAAAAAA AAAAAAAAAAAAAAAAAAAAAAH!'

'AAAAAAAAAAAAAAAAAAAAAAAAAAAAAAAAAAAAAAAAAAAA AAAAAH!' Toby joined in.

The line went dead. Wiping his chest and stomach with tissue paper, Toby tried to recall the voice just now. The American accent struck him as somehow false. Eventually recognition clicked. This was the guy the boss had pointed out as the British Cabinet Minister.

The next phone call was from the boss.

'Okay, Toby, you've done yer stint on the air waves. I want ya in the hall in fifteen minutes. We're gonna do an audition for the movie.'

'Should I wear anything special?' He was remembering his audition for a place at the palace two years ago, when he had to dress up as Tarzan's wild boy.

'Just that pretty silver chair around yer neck and yer ankle bracelet. That's all you'll need. See ya in a mo.'

'Sure, chief! See ya, chief!'

Peter Slater

Chapter Seven

The hall was a scene of chaos. Imagine a cross between a Roman slave auction, a Fellini film set and the antechamber to Paradise.

Boys, naked, painted, dressed in Elizabethan costume and in loin cloths, hung around in groups. Some were reciting lines ('Test me! Test me!'), others were performing acrobatics (the part of Ariel, the fairy servant, seemed as if it might require some gymnastic ability) and others were simply involved in conversations which clearly did not hold their interest, for they were forever glancing towards the stage. On the stage, Sam Greatorix was directing a team of helpers in rolling out a carpet and fixing up lights and sound equipment. Wendell Banks was at the grand piano, strumming an accompaniment to Washington, who was singing 'Moon River'. The black boy, wearing only white gym socks sat on top the piano, leaning back on his hands, legs spread far apart. His cock lay huge and flaccid, nuzzling its own reflection on the polished lid.

'Heya, Toby!' greeted several, as Toby entered the hall. Someone passed him a toke, and he inhaled a good lungful, shaking his head as the vigour of whatever drug it was instantly took effect.

'Gee, Man!' Suddenly, he was floating. He passed through a sea of bodies on his way to the stage. Hands groped, lips kissed and he lingered long for a new boy to deep-tongue kiss him and finger his ass. Toby's anal sphincter was the most sensitive in Arizona. Being rimmed by a quivering tongue was his chief sexual delight, and being stroked by a moist finger also came pretty high up his list of delights. But, for once, there was not the time for prolonged sexual contact. Sam had seen him and was urgently beckoning him to approach the stage.

'Toby, honey,' said Sam, as Toby approached the stage. 'You got the part of Ariel - I knew it as soon as I saw ya walk in. There's no need for you to audition. But I want ya instead ta sit on the audition panel. As one of the major players, you can help choose the other parts - and that's important 'cos you'll be havin' sex with most of 'em. Think you

Paradise Palace

can handle it?'

'Sure!' Toby shrugged and grinned.

'Gee, kid, I like you're smile! - remind me, by the way, that we need some updated photos for our new brochure. I want one of you being rimmed by Washington and sucked by Curt at the same time. Forget Cleopatra - for the face you make at those times, Mark Anthony would have started a World War, never mind a war against a few spaced-out Trojans and their wooden horses. Gimme a kiss and then stroll over to the piano there. I'm putting it about that there's a five thousand dollar reward to the first boy who can get it off with Wendell Banks. Straight up!' he responded to Toby's quizzical look. 'The guy's had a bad experience with boys and he needs ta be reintradooced.'

Toby was not one to hesitate, but, 'Get the fuck out of it!' said Wendell when the boy sat next to him on the piano stool and placed a hand over his crotch.

Toby looked across at Sam and shrugged. Sam mimicked the shrug. And, in that moment, something extraordinary happened. Our lives are full of epiphanies - those moments when the soul seems to turn and a fresh truth is revealed to us unexpectedly.

Seeing Toby's unaffected, cheerful smile, Sam realised that he was in love with the boy. Hell, he loved all the boys; but with Toby it was something special. All the boys would happily make love with him any time, and all would equally agree to read him a poem or two or a chapter of a book. But with the other boys, Sam always had to ask. Toby was the only one among them who volunteer his services. 'Feeling okay, chief?' the boy would enquire. 'How about a fuck? - it's been a slow day so far.' Or, perhaps, the boy would ring through to Sam's office - as he had done only last week - 'Hey, chief, I'm in the library and I've just discovered some guy called T.S. Eliot. I'd love to read ya one of these poems while you jerk me off. You free for a while?' But it was not only the sexual favours that Sam appreciated. He simply liked to have the kid around. Sam always slept alone and, lately, before drifting off to sleep (clutching the Ken Barbie doll that was the greatest

Peter Slater

secret in a palace full of secrets), he thought of Toby. Had he wanted him for sex, he could, of course, have rung for him and the boy would have appeared immediately. But it wasn't that. It wasn't that at all.

Toby moved away from the piano and his gaze met Sam's for that crucial extra beat.

Sam looked away with a rueful shake of his head. Heck, what was he doing? He was an old man. Not too old for good sex, but a darn sight too old to be falling in love like a teenager.

Sam handed out the revised scripts to all the boys and the auditions began.

Sam, Wendell, Toby and Jed sat on chairs in the main body of the hall and the boys climbed onto the stage, one by one, two by two or three by three (according to the requirements of their chosen scenes), and gave their all. The beauty of their bodies was undeniable, and those parts of the stage direction which called for sexual action were well-performed; but otherwise the general quality of their acting and delivery of their lines was appalling.

'A fish would have spoken those words with more emotion!' complained Sam to one hapless boy, who had stumbled haltingly over one of the greatest speeches in Elizabethan literature.

'Then get a fish!' protested the boy, who had gone to great trouble to dress in doublet and hose. He tore the feather cap from his head and flung it to the ground.

The small drama planted an idea in the mind of one of the more elderly visitors to the palace. Within a week he would be making love to this boy in a crate filled with a thousand cod, salmon, trout and squid.

Apart from a moment here, a moment there, casting was a pretty dull and dispiriting business.

'Are you sure you want to go ahead with this project?' Sam asked Wendell when it was all over.

'Sure!' Wendell appeared surprised by the question. 'I think we're auditioning by different standards, here, Sam baby. You're looking for style and quality, I'm looking for what my public want - length of cock,

Paradise Palace

width of pecs and facial expression. And don't get on yer high horse! - you're the same when you're looking for boys to take on at the palace.'

'But this is different. I would have thought that in a Shakespeare film one would have hoped for a little artistic integrity.'

'Balls! One is looking for a little cock integrity, and that's about it.'

'But isn't it a shame that this won't then turn out to be anything other than just a run-of-the-mill porno flick?'

'Oh, it'll be different. The staging, the music, the lighting... And look at it this way - the main parts will be superbly played. Me as Prospero, you as Caliban, Toby here as Ariel, Jed as Ferdinand. And not all your boys were horrible. That Washington, he was good. He'd make a good Sebastian. What d'ya reckon, Toby? As you'll see, we've written in a few extra scenes where Ariel flies in and seduces Sebastian, who, up till when he sees you, has always resisted gay advances. The first scene is Act Three, Scene Two. Sebastian is sleeping in a shady bower - cue exotic birdsong, the rush of the sea - when he feels something lightly brush across his face. He thinks it's a fly at first, and twitches his nose and shakes his sleeping head. But then, when it persists, he raises his hand to swat the dratted thing and he finds it ain't a fly at all but the tip of your cock as you hover right above him...'

'And I get to sing my song, right?' said Toby.

'Right!'

'"Where the bee sucks, there suck I:
In a cowslip's bell I lie;
There I couch when owls do cry... "'

Toby spoke in a voice as mellifluous and airy as sunlight itself.

Sam sighed.

'And,' Wendell continued. 'You get to do the whole sex scene whilst still suspended on a rope. In fact, I think you get to do all your scenes whilst suspended. Ya see, Sam, it's this sorta thing that's gonna make our movie distinguished. There'll be poetry beautifully spoke by

– 35 –

Peter Slater

those of us who are up to it, and the rest will be ingenious invention. No-one'll notice there's one or two of the boys whose acting don't quite match up to Royal Skakespeare standards. How about you, Jed? You been real quiet, so far. Got any opinions?'

But Jed Howitzer, whose knowledge and appreciation of great Art did not extend much beyond lewd cave paintings from the Auvergne and dodgy Greek vases, had chosen to make the ultimate artistic statement: he was fast asleep.

Chapter Eight

Something was happening to Sam Greatorix. That night he could not sleep. He lay between the cool silk sheets of his four-poster bed and tossed and turned. He was deeply tired, but sleep would not come. He tried counting sheep, thinking of clouds and imagining himself as a train driver speeding through a dark tunnel; but none of these things would trip the sleep mechanism in his brain.

His problem was Toby. He could not get the boy out of his mind. He heard his voice reciting poetry, talking about Walt Whitman or merely offering chit-chat. He saw that sweet smile and graceful figure. He remembered the delicate kiss of his lips. He needed that boy so badly… But it was more complicated than that. He more than wanted him. This was not simple lust, as we have observed before. Simple lust was easily assuaged at the palace. A press of the button beside his bed and Toby would be with him in five minutes. Great. He would be with him. But what did that mean? Nothing. Oh, it satisfied a temporary lust and eased a passing moment; but Sam wanted and needed something deeper. He was in love with the boy, and he wanted that love to be reciprocated. He wanted the boy to see that he, Sam, was not merely another man needing sexual release. He wanted the boy to appreciate him for his qualities: his sensibility, his conversation, his essential good spirit. He was more than a cock and balls needing massage and sexual release. He was one who loved and who wanted to be loved in turn.

But how does love come about? Sam, for all his worldly experience, had no idea: he had never experienced the thing before. Indeed, he had been highly cynical about the emotion. 'Love is a neurosis,' he had often quoted William Burroughs with approval. Love was an indulgence and an irrelevance. A comfort blanket for the insecure. Money and sex were all a man needed.

Oh, perhaps this business with Toby was merely a sexual obsession. Perhaps he should just press his bell right now, get the boy to come. They would have excellent sex and then he would be able to get

Peter Slater

to sleep and by morning all this silliness would be forgotten...

But something held him back. Press the bell, Sam, press the bell, urged a voice inside his head. But no. He didn't want to do that. He didn't want to lose this feeling he had, and if keeping his hands off the boy helped retain the feeling, then that was what he must do. Was it a pleasant feeling, then? Sleeplessness and a nebulous ache? No, outwardly it was very uncomfortable; but somehow, he sensed deep inside him, there was something else. Something pure and good. He couldn't quite access it fully yet, only sensed that it was there. But he wanted to hang on to it - was, in fact, terrified of losing it.

Inner debate, however, was no way to encourage sleep. He loathed the very idea of pills, so they were not an option. What he needed, he decided, was a tantric massage.

He switched on the bedside lamp. Oh, god, it was 3 a.m., that most desolate of all times - and a busy time for the boys, who could expect calls from clients wanting teddy bears brought to them or bedtime stories read to them. The library at the palace was well stocked with fairy tale classics and numerous editions of Alice in Wonderland. Mae, the only boy with true transvestite qualities, was frequently asked to dress up as Mama. In the depths of the night, the merchant bankers, heads of multi-nationals, politicians and chat-show hosts often found themselves with a desperate need to relocate their lost childhoods. In the lost childhood of Judas, Christ was betrayed - so, perhaps, the Paradise therapy made some difference, not only to its clients, but also to the world at large.

Sam pressed the bell.

'Paradise night desk, Curt speaking. How can we help you, sir?' came a disembodied voice.

'Curt, sweetheart, it's Sam here. Is Washington around? I'm in need of a massage.'

'I'm afraid he's not, chief - he was called out to room 24 about an hour ago. How about Toby? - he's free, and he gives a good massage.'

'NO!' Sam almost shouted. 'I don't want goddamn Toby.' He quieted. 'I'm sorry, Curt. I wanted Washingtom, especially, because he's the only one trained in the tantric arts and that's what I was looking for, this night. Look, if he comes back in the next half hour, and if he doesn't look in too bad a way, could you ask him to pop round to me?'

'Sure thing, chief. Anything else? A little night-cap, maybe?'

'Nah... Oh, on second thoughts, get someone to bring me round a Southern Comfort.'

'It's on its way, chief.'

'Well done, Curt.'

Sam switched off the intercom, sighed and picked up the book beside his bed. It was David Copperfield - an old, old favourite, he had read it many times. Re-reading such a book was like renewing acquaintanceship with old friends. There they all were: Mr Micawber, Uriah Heep, Betsy Trotwood, Traddles, Davy himself...

Sam made himself comfortable on his pillows, opened the book and took up where he left off. Suddenly, unaccountably, he found his eyes filling with tears: it was so pleasant to be once again with all these characters in Victorian England, and yet there was also a certain sadness here. After a while, Sam laid the book down and gazed at a point in the middle distance. And, for the first time in his life, he realised that he was lonely.

Meanwhile, in another room, on another floor - indeed in another, far-flung wing of the palace - Morpheus, that sly boy-god of sleep, was again playing hard to get. Wendell Banks was also troubled by love. He was not alone, he had Jed with him; but Jed could not satisfy his post-coital needs, which ran to far more than a simple cigarette. Goddamn it, he wanted to discuss myth, magic and metaphor in Wagner's Ring cycle, and Jed wouldn't know what Wagner's Ring was if it upped and mugged him on the New York subway.

'When you get to a certain age you need something to get yer teeth into,' he complained to Jed.

'What's wrong with this!?' With characteristic lumpen crudity, Jed rose up and in a single deft movement lowered his massive cock and balls over the face of the troubled director, who spat and shook his head violently from side to side.

'Will you get outa here? That's not what I meant at all! In fact you boys are the opposite of what I want - I don't know why I succumbed, just now. All boys can give is an irritating irritation of the genitals that results in a spasm of greater or lesser pleasure - and that's it. I've been there, done that. Now I want something else.'

'Gee, boss!'

'Don't "Gee, boss" me, like some gormless halfwit punk. Tell me what ya think of Jung.'

'Young Who?'

'Jeez! Kids these days! Didn't they teach ya nothin in school? Carl Gustav Jung, the great philosopher and psychoanalyst.'

'Oh, sure. Him.'

'Yeah. Him.'

Silence, heavy and awkward as a sexually-aroused hippopotamus clambering out of a waterhole.

Then, 'You in love, boss?'

'No!' snapped Wendell.

'Boss, I've known you for over five years. I can tell your mood, boss. I've only ever once seen you like this before, and that was when you had that crush on President Clinton's Press Secretary. I think you're in love.'

'I am not, goddamn, in goddamn love!'

'With Sam Greatorix. Admit it, boss. You're in love with the guy. This isn't just a passing lust. You got it bad.'

'Why is it, Jed?' Feeling himself succumb to the truth, Wendell experienced an enormous flood of relief. A rogue part of his mind imagined himself floating out on the warm Pacific on an air mattress. The mind is its own place. 'Why love? All these weird chemical and electrical impulses in our bodies... why aren't we always completely satisfied with just fucking anyone - even if, in the homosexual act, it must always, perforce, be a simulacrum of the true act of mating?'

Wendell could load a mean sentence full of clauses in the way

Paradise Palace

that a thug might fill a hollow cosh with nuts, screws and nails.

'I dunno, boss,' replied the dazed Jed.

'Of course you "dunno" because you're a dummy. Aw, I'm sorry - you don't deserve harsh words. I'm in a state of mental distress. He loves me, he loves me not - why the "not"?'

Jed might have said that forty years - and much more - had besieged Wendell's brow, that was why. But he merely observed, 'Because Sam's a man who likes his boys, that's why. Gee, boss, if there weren't types like him, you and me would never be able to make the living that we do. God bless 'em all.'

'People can change, though, can't they? Force of circumstance, experience, other people can make them change. All great literature is about change. Art is about change and the possibility of change. In change is hope. You gotta roll away the rock from the cave door.'

'You're gettin' too obscure for me, boss.'

'The cave is the mind. You have to free the mind. Sam's trapped in lust for boys. He needs to find a more mature approach to the problems of the flesh.'

Strange words indeed from the wealthiest maker of pornographic movies in the Western world. But these were strange times.

'I don't think it's just that, boss,' said Jed. 'In Sam's case, it's also something else.'

'Whaddaya mean?'

'Well, I've been watching him pretty closely, these past few days…'

'So have I, so have I!'

'And have ya noticed anything?'

'Beyond his beauty and the beauty of his intellect?'

'Yeah.'

Wendell shook his head. 'No, can't say I have.'

'That's because you've been blinded by love,' said Jed, digging out the only fragment of philosophy that he had managed to gather in his twenty-five years. 'But my mind's been clear,' he continued, tapping his mind as if he expected the hollow sound of clarity. 'I've been a disinterested observer, so to speak, and I've seen something else. Quite something else.'

'Spit it out!' Wendell was becoming exasperated. As a film director he was fond of the slow build-up, but not in every situation of the human comedy.

'Sam Great-or-ix is in love. Himself.'

'Sam Greatorix is in love with himself? - Well, tell me somethin' new!'

'No, no. He's himself in love. Like you.'

'He's in love with me?' Wendell grasped Jed's cock and began rhythmically to press it.

'Uh, uh, sorry Boss. He's in love with one of his boys. I'm surprised you haven't noticed.'

'Sure I've noticed! But not love. I've noticed lust all over his face. He lusts after all of them.'

'This is more than that, boss. This is L O V E .'

'With whom?' The horrid green serpent of jealousy was stirring in his belly. He could feel its slow trickling movement deep inside.

'Can't you guess?'

'Any more play acting and I'll fire you on the spot.'

He had not noticed that Jed's cock had grown huge beneath his pulsing fingers.

'Toby. The pretty, blond-haired one. The one who sat on the audition panel between you and me.'

In a moment, all was apparent. Horror-struck, Wendell let go of Jed's cock and sank back dazed. After an age, he spoke: 'Fuck me until I beg for mercy, Jed. And then some. Don't stop until you've broken every sensitive nerve in my body.'

Jed, already fully aroused, needed no urging.

The evil green serpent might have smiled.

A knock at the door, and Swing and Swung, the Native American boys, entered. They wore only loincloths, and their faces were streaked with war-paint. Swing carried a tray on which stood a glass, a beaker of ice cubes and a bottle of Southern Comfort.

Sam laid down his book and smiled.

'Thanks, boys. Put the tray down on the table, here. Why don't you join me in a glass?'

They shook their heads.

'Sorry - you're teetotal, I know. I respect you for that. A man's gotta have some morals. Stay awhile, though. Keep me company. I'm having trouble sleeping, here.

The dark-skinned boys, smooth and flowing as oil, slid onto the bed and lay on either side of Sam. They adopted the comforting stillness of cats.

'That's my boys! When ya get to my age, ya need company sometimes of a night. All sorts of imaginary monsters, like you wouldn't believe, start to try and come and get you. You start to wonder what it's all about. What are we doing? Why are we here? Why do we spend so much of our precious energy on chasing a few moments of sensual pleasure? Why is a poem not enough? Beethoven's E minor string quartet? My god, that should be all a man needs for the rest of his life! But it isn't. I don't know why.

'You Native Americans, you had your music, your stories, your hunting... you were more balanced before the white man came along. I guess I'm sorry for what we all did to you... Did you guys have love out there on the plains and in the forests? I guess you did. I read somewhere that certain tribes believed that their gay brethren were in touch with all things sacred, and that they held elevated rank as witch-doctors or medicine men. To be gay was to be something honoured and revered - you loved not merely for the procreation of the race but just for the sake of love itself. I think we've forgotten that, somehow. Maybe the Paradise Palace is too obsessed with the frankly erotic... What d'ya think, boys?'

Well, the boys might have thought a thousand and one things, and all fascinating, but none was to be revealed that night: they were asleep.

Apprehending a further infusion of dread loneliness, Sam

trembled like an aspen leaf. But then was still. Something of the calm understanding of the Native American spirit seeped into his own soul from the presence of these two good boys, and a certain peace began to seep through his veins. Peace, and its lovely, welcome companion, Sleep. Sleep, certain knot of peace…

Soon, the room held only three quiet souls and dreams of hunters running naked through the dark forests of the night.

Chapter Nine

When Sam Greatorix awoke the next morning, he was, initially, cheerful. He lay in his bed and listened to the mellifluous fluting of the Koel birds (specially imported from India) in the branches of the flame tree (specially imported from Thika) outside his window. These birds had the loveliest voices of all creatures, and visitors often mistook their song for the tolling of bells in the wind. He heard, too, the splashing of water from either plant sprinklers or one of the many fountains positioned around the grounds. In the desert, nothing lifts the human heart quite so much as the sound of water; and, seeking the happiness of all who came here, Sam had paid much attention to that piece of human psychology by ensuring that water was everywhere to be seen and heard. Happily, the Paradise Palace was positioned above inexhaustible artesian wells, and geologists had confidently predicted that it would be a hundred years before anything approaching a water shortage might present a problem. Sam's happiness was not merely dependent on this aural stimulation, however. The sweet presence of the two Indian boys also played its part. Their perfect bodies were stretched out on either side of him, forming a guard of unassailable beauty.

Sam imagined the birds in the trees, hopping along the branches in dappled sunlight, flying over the green sward, drinking at one of the ponds, where goldfish swam in clear water beneath flowering water-lilies, and a blue dragonfly darted across the surface, with sharply dipping movements). He thought, 'If I could stay like this forever I would be happy forever. Just breathing. Happiness comes when you can be content with merely staying still. It's all this moving about that is so destructive.'

Because, this morning, he knew, in an as yet unacknowledged part of his mind, that once he moved, once he started about the business of the day, this feeling of contentment would disappear as fast as dew in sunlight.

He raised himself slightly, looked first at one boy and then at the other. They were both lying face down, deep in the sleep of the just.

He lay back, and it was gone. No more the peace of the Koel birds and water. There in his mind hovered the picture of Toby - and, far worse, not just Toby, but Toby making love with another boy. Then Toby fellating a man, Toby fucking a man, a man rimming Toby and Toby's face a tight grimace of pained pleasure.

Sam groaned. All was lost. Pascal once wrote that all man's troubles came from him not being able to confine himself to one room. All well and good; but if Pascal had been a gaoler and had locked Sam up in his suite at the Paradise, Sam would have been driven to desperate suicide. He had to get out, and quick.

Taking care not to waken the boys, he slid down the centre of the bed, making no more disturbance than a heavy breath. After a quick shower, he dressed and set out to face the world.

It was 10 a.m., but such a time had a pre-dawn air at the Paradise, where nights generally ran to excess and mornings, by and large, did not exist for the majority of guests and boys. Sam walked through a sleeping palace to his office. Lost time was fine for his staff and clients, but the manager of a successful enterprise could not afford to spend his mornings asleep.

Once inside his office, Sam took the unusual step of locking the door. Then he sat at his desk and began to work through all the faxes and e-mails that had come in overnight from all over the world. There were enquiries from prospective guests, offers from film-makers, job applications and a request from a man who had recently stayed at the palace for three boys to make up a ship's crew sailing the South Pacific in a couple of months. This last annoyed Sam. There was a notice pinned in every room that none of the boys was free for work outside of the palace, ever. He couldn't bear poachers, and each boy's contract recorded this.

Fax, phone and e-mail were the palace's main means of contact with

Paradise Palace

the outside world: a post van called by once a fortnight (at great expense, that involved not only money but sexual favours for the head of the local post depot); but, obviously, those who wanted a speedier response had to communicate other than by letter.

As he worked, he drank coffee and smoked cigarettes.

An hour passed. Occasionally the phone rang or the fax belched out another message; but otherwise all was quiet and Sam's head was filled with nothing but work and the demands of work.

Then at 11.30, apparently apropos of nothing at all, Sam stood up, removed his clothes and walked across to the end wall of the office. There, drilled into the brick work were handcuffs at a height of about six feet, a neck-brace not much lower and leg cuffs a foot from the ground. Sam locked himself into the leg cuffs, balancing on tiny ledges which, following a kick, slid back into the wall; then with a dexterity born of infinite practise clamped his neck into the rubber noose and both his wrists into the handcuffs. Then he waited in silence for pain.

Of course, Sam, like many of the guests, was not averse to a touch of masochism now and again. He loved to be tied and soundly thrashed; and, very occasionally, he would indulge in a piece of delicate genital torture, weighing down his balls with lead and piercing his cock with pins. There was also a slightly risky game involving ropes and near-asphyxiation that, for some reason, he generally liked to play on his birthdays.

But there was a difference between those games and what he was doing now. In those games there were always others present. There were clearly-defined boundaries and help was at hand should a speedy release be called for. Now, hanging from the wall, behind a locked door, there was no prospect of release. The pain would slowly grow and grow, pass through the domain of pleasure and enter a truly awful region. Sam wanted this with all his heart.

A dull grey ache spread down his arms...

Why did Sam want this? Why was he doing this terrible thing to himself? Surely his was not an unrequited love? He was not the man who gazes from afar and can never hope to gain the bed of a great

Peter Slater

beauty. Far from it. He could have sex with Toby whenever he so chose. He could have Toby's company all the livelong day. But what he did not have, and what he believed deep down he could never hope to have, was Toby's love. This was not merely because he was some fifty years older than Toby - although, perforce, that factor played its part. No, it was due to the fact that Sam - dear old confident, loveable Sam - believed that no-one, truly, could fall in love with him. He had never been loved. Even as a child.

His right small toe cramped slightly and began to pulse independently...

On a winter's night in 1949, in New York City, an office clerk, hurrying home from work, had heard a faint wailing coming from a garbage can. Finding, on closer investigation, a child therein, he backed away. This was not his business, hell no. He didn't want to get involved. Besides, he was hungry, and his wife would be putting dinner on the table. Continuing his homeward course, the clerk congratulated himself on his strong resolution. Think of all the difficulties and confusion and sheer damn nuisance he had just got himself out of! The police, ambulances, doctors, newspapermen... Hell, he would never have gotten home! Oh, sure, there might have been some nice publicity: HERO CLERK SAVES CHILD! On the other hand, perhaps things might not quite have worked out like that. People were so suspicious, untrusting and cynical, these days, they might have suspected him of trying to murder the baby: CLERK ATTEMPTS MURDER OF LOVE CHILD! SEARCH ON FOR MOTHER!

His arms began to prickle with pins and needles: he imagined a myriad tiny white spots flourishing beneath his skin...

The baby was eventually rescued by an alcoholic panhandler searching for scraps of food. For a week, he kept the child in his basement squat in The Bronx: it was a cute sort of toy, a pastime. He fed it flat beer and bread that he first chewed up in his own mouth. In the end, however, he got sick and tired of the brat's constant wailing and dumped him on the steps of a police station. Sam was named after the police captain who found him the next morning. The baby was more

Paradise Palace

dead than alive, suffering from malnutrition, alcohol poisoning and hypothermia. It spent most of its first year in hospital before being sent to The Nazareth Home for Orphan Children. Run by a near psychopathic monomaniac, the place was more state penitentiary than home, however. Sam had an unhappy childhood.

Pain began in earnest after about half an hour. Silver knives ran along the edge of muscles, nerves twisted and pulled...

Sam's history, then, was based on rejection. He experienced no love and was taught no concept of love. He never associated the sexual act with love. You had sex with someone because you desired their body: there could be no other reason. As a teenager he desired men and women and made love with many; but this was never "love" in any romantic sense. Of course, he had read about "love" and seen it portrayed in the movies. But fiction was not life. Stories were stories.

Pain was the universe. The brain grew confused by the signals of agony it was receiving from its remotest body parts and it interpreted the agony as the tearing of flesh, the pulling back of skin by knives to expose raw nerves. Twisting and turning, he involuntarily tightened the noose around his neck. He could scarcely breathe...

But now, for the first time in his life, for the first time in fifty years, Sam was touched by a sensation he had hitherto never acknowledged by so much as a single serious thought. And he did not understand. He was as confused as a teenager. Moreover, because he had never once been shown love, either as a child or an adult, he could not believe that he could ever be its recipient. So, instead, he chose pain, which was far more tangible and something that he could understand.

Pain flowed through him as inexorably as blood. It was like molten metal, and Sam knew a terrible joy borne of this intimation of the closeness of mortality...

...amor: love...

...mors: death...

...the two walk hand in hand.

Sam waits.

Hours pass.

Peter Slater

Hours passed.

Hours passed and no-one came for Sam - the small boy locked in his cell-like room by a cruel matron.

Hours passed and no-one came for Sam - the millionaire entrepreneur hanging naked from a wall in his office and unable to free himself.

But, ultimately, the Paradise Palace was a close community, and no-one could go missing for long. Indeed, because of the nature of some of the exercises on offer to the guests it was imperative that regular checks were made on all. Only last year, a certain Reinhardt Kobler, head of a merchant bank and reputedly the richest man in Germany, had been reported as not having been seen for several hours and was found in his bath in a crotchless rubber suit splashed with cum and wearing a rubber Ronald Reagan mask. His particular delight was to orgasm whilst the supply of oxygen to the brain was strictly limited. Luckily, he was reached just in time and he and the Germany economy were saved to fight another day.

It was Wendell Banks who kicked the door down - not that there was any need for that, Curt had found a spare key, but Wendell liked a dramatic statement. He had been searching high and low for Sam - hell, he needed his help in finding places where they might start filming. The camera crew and lighting boys were due at the palace later that day.

'Sam, what the fuck?' were Wendell's first words as he hurtled into the room followed by a curious train of naked boys. 'Yer nicely-hung, though!' he admired, mincing towards Sam in characteristic tiny steps. He took out his cigar and plugged his mouth over Sam's cock. Then, remembering himself, he took a step backwards. 'Gee, you're not well, fella! How long've ya been like this? You're as pale as death. A man can go too far with this sex play business, ya know. And locking yerself in is darned dangerous. Where's the keys to the cuffs?'

Sam was far gone. He could only whisper, 'It's all over!'

Wendell took efficient command. He had always fancied himself as a battlefield commander in the Civil War (indeed, in his movie

Soldier Boy - subtitled The Blue and the Grey - he had played the part of General Schofield, the only black gay general on the Confederate side, who fell in love with a brave drummer boy). Imagining himself on a high knoll, he shouted, 'Search for the keys!' in the tone of voice that an ancestor might have used for such a phrase as 'Avenge Williamsburg!'

Such high drama was not strictly necessary. Curt found the keys easily enough on top of the desk. He was the one to free Sam. Who fell into the arms of Washington and Toby. And, such is the way of these things, Sam deliberately laid most of his weight and got most comfort and delight from Washington. Indeed, Toby might have had reason to feel snubbed.

They laid Sam out on the floor, and Doctor Max Martin was called. The good doctor, whose answer to most of the ills at the palace that were not obviously sexually transmitted was to prescribe a sedative and brandy, did not break this habit now. He injected Sam with a heavy dose of morphine, gave him a swig from a bottle of Courvoisier and told the boys to take him off to bed.

'He's been overworking, that's all. The guy just needs a good rest.'

His wise insight was backed-up by Curt, who related the incident of the night before.

Chapter Ten

'So what does this tell us, fella?'

Wendell and Jed were walking in the Italian Garden. This was an area of low box-hedges, gravel paths, flower beds, ponds, statues, and topiary hedges, cut in the shapes of birds and boys,. The statues were gold and, needless to say, were of naked youths. Large blue butterflies and colourful dragonflies abounded.

'It's proof positive,' said Jed. 'Sam's in love with the kid, Toby, and the kid don't love him.'

'How'd ya know the kid don't love him?'

'Because he's a hunderd an' ninety and the kid's eighteen. It figures.'

'I think you're exaggerating, but let it pass, let it pass. What d'ya think'll happen next?'

'He might just pine away and die...'

'Or?'

'The kid might fall in love with him and they live happily ever after.'

'Or?'

'He might just forget the kid after a while.'

'Or?'

'What's with all these "ors"?'

'You're not giving me the dream alternative.'

'What's that, boss?'

'Sam falls in love with me, and we live happily ever after.'

'Dream on, boss, dream on.'

'You've got a hard heart for one so young, Jed. A real hard heart.'

'It could happen, I suppose,' conceded Jed.

'What've I told you before, kid, about overdoing the subjunctive? You gotta look for the positive and think positive. No "ifs" or "coulds" - that's not the American way.'

'But to be positive, you gotta have hope and reason for hope. Where's the reason in what you're saying, boss?'

Paradise Palace

'My positive hope is based on a solid foundation of sure reason. And I'll tell ya what that is. Sam Greatorix is in love with one boy, right?'

'Right.'

'That means he's getting jaded with boys per se. At one time, I'll bet he was happy as a sandboy to sleep with a different boy every night - it didn't matter who, he loved all the boys just the same. But now he's changing. Boys, and the easy availability of boys, are becoming boring. Don't I know it myself? The same thing happened to me! So he focuses on one. Put it this way. Last year, I might have had twenty rivals for Sam's heart. Now there's only one.'

'What are you trying to say, boss?'

'I want Toby taken out. I want him no longer to exist.'

'You want him dead, boss?'

'That's one alternative. That would be very satisfactory. But there are other ways of getting rid of people.'

'Such as?'

'I buy him out. I'm going to offer him ten thousand dollars to leave this place and never show his ugly mug around here again. And when he's gone, who d'ya think will be on hand to comfort poor lonesome Sam and to read him T.S. Eliot and Shakespeare sonnets? I'll seduce him with sweet poetry, worldly wisdom and my massive genitals, in a way that no mere boy could hope to emulate. What d'ya reckon, Jed? You're my confidant in all this. My one true friend.'

'Go for it, boss!'

'Do ya think it'll work?'

'When have you ever failed, boss?' was as much affirmation as honest Jed could offer.

But it was enough.

'When have I ever failed? When have I ever failed?' Wendell repeated. And the answer came back: 'Never.'

Whilst Wendell's mind was tight with scheming, Sam's was loose amongst weird morphine dreams. He was an angel, clad in scarlet robes and drifting through clouds. Ahead of him, always just ahead,

Peter Slater

was another angel - Toby. Toby was naked, but nothing could be seen of him - other than the odd tantalising glimpse of chest, buttock or thigh - because he was wreathed in cloud. Sam kept reaching out to catch the boy, but it was impossible. It was impossible to get up any speed up here in the heavens. You strove to move swiftly, but movement was forever denied.

The dream changed and Sam was racing along behind a horse ridden by a naked boy. The horse's hooves splashed mud on the man and the man was thankful for the indignity...

Now he was in the ocean, swimming after a merboy...

Now on another planet - all desert, craters and a large green moon emerging from behind a mountain - in pursuit of the blue Orgasm Kid...

'Toby, Toby, Toby...' Sam groaned in his sleep.

It was not Toby on duty at that particular moment in Sam's delirium, however; but Washington.

'Toby, I want Toby!' Sam opened his eyes.

'He can't come, chief. He's with a client.'

Sam's look, then, was so full of horror, that Washington hastened to reassure, 'But he'll be through in a couple of hours. I'll get a message to him to tell him to come over to you straight away.'

Sam attempted to get up, and Washington had forcibly to restrain him.

'Doctor's orders. He said on no account was you to get up. You gotta recover, chief.'

'Where's Toby? Who's he with?'

'Frank Grunwitz - the biscuit man from Arkansas.'

'No way am I gonna let him stay with that punk!' He struggled again to rise.

'No, chief! Don't! You're delirious!'

'I'm gonna go in there and tear that Frank Grunwitz limb from limb. I'll teach him to clutch onto my Toby like the fat mating toad he is!'

'Calm down, chief! Please! You'll regret it so much if you go barging in on the guests. Word'll get round and the business will never recover!'

'Business? Who cares about business? That's the American curse! Love is the only thing that matters in this world.'

He struggled yet more fiercely. But he was no match for Washington and eventually sank back exhausted and defeated. He closed his eyes and the dreams returned.

When Toby returned to his room from having serviced Frank Grunwitz, he was deadbeat and in need of a shower and a good sleep. Mr Grunwitz had fantasies concerning chocolate, cream and lemon cakes; and, although Toby found them all good fun, they left him feeling rather nauseous.

The answering machine behind his bed was winking its red light:

'Aah, Toby, baby. Wendell Banks here. I'd like to make you an offer you can't refuse. Can you come and see me as soon as you get back? You won't regret it, I promise.'

Toby received offers he "could not refuse" just about every day of his life so, although he made a note of this one, he would not bother visiting Mr Banks until that evening.

The next message was from Washington:

'Toby. The chief's in a bad way. He's been asking for you. Can you pop round when you're free?'

Toby sat on the side of the bed and held his head in his hands. Should he go and see the chief right away? He knew that he ought to; but, frankly, he was so tired he just did not feel up to it. No. That one could be put on hold as well. It was a decision that he was to live to regret.

Toby took a languorous shower and dried himself inside the warm air booth with which each room at the palace was equipped. Then he turned the ringer on his phone off and plugged his ears with wax. Goodbye, world. Within ten minutes he was stretched between white cotton sheets and shivering deliciously into a deep baby sleep. If anyone were to investigate Toby's dreams, he would find only clocks and clouds.

Peter Slater

Hours passed. Sam bobbed in and out of consciousness. 'Is he here yet?' he would ask, the dying Polish King hoping to set eyes one last time on his long lost son, the Prince of Warsaw.

And always, Washington or Curt would look up from computer game or book and say, quietly, 'Not yet, chief. Not yet.'

'Why won't he come? You've left a message? He knows I'm asking for him?'

'We've rung him several times, and been round to his room - there's no answer. You know that Frank Grunwitz, he can keep a boy for hours with his chocolate and lemon torte.

Doctor Max looked in from time to time. On one occasion, Sam was particularly distressed and tears were rolling down his cheeks, so the doctor gave him another powerful shot of sedative.

Notwithstanding all the high drama at the heart of the palace, life and love went on unabated in all the other various parts of its body.

Midway through that afternoon, something appeared out of the East. From a distance it appeared nothing more than a strangely hovering black speck caught between the harsh blue of the sky and the brown of the desert. Gradually, however, it took on the aspect of a weirdly malevolent insect growing ever larger as it approached its destination.

Father Paul, the mild-mannered priest from Wisconsin, was the first to see it. He was sitting in a hammock slung between two palm trees, sipping a Pina Colada and quietly pondering the paradoxes of Immanuel Kant, when he happened to look up.

The flying machine was still some distance away, but its destination was apparent. It seemed to Father Paul that it was heading straight for him. This was the promised vengeance of the Lord that he had feared at the back of his mind from the first hour of his stay at the Palace.

Vengeance is mine and I will repay, saith the Lord. Suddenly, this and a host of other related phrases and words of kindly warning came sailing through Father Paul's mind: "Fire", "burn", "plague", "smote",

Paradise Palace

"eternity"... "And there came out of the smoke locusts upon the earth: and unto them was given power, as the scorpions of the earth have power..."

Father Paul lost his thirst for the Pina Colada. The glass dropped from his trembling hand and he tumbled from the hammock, got down onto his knees and began to pray. This was the most terrible moment he had ever experienced - worse, even, than that time when, preaching the sermon at his first church, his motorised butt-plug (with which he was permanently fitted back then) started to life of its own accord.

'Get me out of this one, Lord, and I'll never look at another boy again,' he promised.

Well, really. One should never make rash promises in the heat of the moment. Did Father Paul really believe that this was an avenging Angel winging its way across the desert? Did the silly fool think that the god who had conveniently overlooked Hitler, Stalin and a host of blood-thirsty generals for so long would really trouble to dispatch Nemesis to a priest whose only 'crime' was to love others of his own sex? Well, yes, he did. The human mind is a curious thing, and people will often work themselves into a state over comparative trifles. Most wars start for no good reason, and... But to get back to death's dark angel...

It was a helicopter.

The sweet silence of the desert was shattered by appalling noise as the great machine landed on a stretch of road, just outside the gates of the palace. A great cloud of dust all but obscured it altogether. Clutching a floppy hat and a large briefcase, out jumped a figure who, dodging the rotor blades in rather melodramatic manner, headed for safety in a sort of crouching Cossack dance step.

The helicopter took off as soon as its passenger was well clear. Its pilot might have fancied himself back in 'Nam, landing troops in the heart of enemy territory.

And now we can see the passenger more clearly as he stands to wave farewell to the pilot. A tall figure in a long blue coat. A shock of blond hair falls from beneath a blue floppy hat, like hay escaping from a windblown stack. The face is sharp and heavily made-up, the features not unlike those of Marlene Dietrich.

The figure now turned to the welcoming committee of dusty naked studs. 'I never know whether to give those guys a tip or not,' were his first words, spoken in rich velvet tones. 'Judy Garbo, legal adviser to the stars,' he held out his heavily-beringed hand. 'I was invited by Jed Howitzer.'

Aaron, who, in the absence of Sam, had assumed the role of acting manager, escorted Judy through the portcullis gate, over the drawbridge (boys and tame sharks swam in the salt-water moat) and across the wide front lawn to the waiting room.

Judy was a compulsive chatterer: 'Gosh, it's hot here! No wonder all you boys go around nude. Do you know, I've only ever once seen such a collection of lovely boys and that was at the country house of the most famous straight actor in Hollywood. Again, I was there on business - only last year, in fact - and just guess how many of our famous moral majority politicians also happened to be visiting? My, my, it's a feast for the eye! I had to sign a contract binding me to secrecy, of course, and not only that: it was made abundantly clear to me that if I should shed so much as a couple of drops of a leak to the media, I would never see my balls again.

'Well, between you and me, I'm planning to say farewell to my balls, anyway. I'm going to have a little party after their removal. I'm not sure how it's going to be yet, though. I may place them on a stand in the centre of the banqueting table, a revolving stand with a spotlight focused on it. Or I may offer them cooked up in a stew... Or maybe in a bowl of peeled grapes as part of a sort of forfeit game. Every time you lose your forfeit would be to plunge your hand into the bowl, sight unseen, and pick out and eat the first thing you touch.

'Oh, golly, I'm rambling! My, what a pretty place you have here! How much do you charge?'

'Thousand dollars a night.'

'Ve-ry reasonable. Extras?'

'There's no extras. Everything's all in. A guest can have anything he wants from chocolate chip cookie ice cream to a Keanu Reeves

Paradise Palace

lookalike at two in the morning.'

'Heh, heh, heh! Very droll!' Judy laughed in extraordinary manner by throwing back his head and castaneting his teeth together in rapid motion - the sound was eerily wooden. 'Heh, heh, heh, heh,' came the chuckle, and clack-clack, clack-clack-clack! went the teeth.

They entered through frosted glass doors and into the reception-area-cum-waiting-room - all potted plants, padded sofas and armchairs, with paintings of boys on the walls. Aaron went behind the desk and produced the visitors book.

'I'll need to sign you in and complete a few formalities,' he said. 'I should explain that we're quite used to having people who come professionally to assist our clients - lawyers, brokers, heart surgeons, and so on - and we usually offer them free accommodation for so long as their work takes. How long do you think you'll be staying?'

'Honey, I've got absolutely no idea! How could I? Jed Howitzer - for whom I've worked several times previously in similar circumstances - has called me to aid with a certain, shall we say, testamentary difficulty,' (his teeth positively clattered on release of this happy turn of phrase) 'and it may take a couple of hours, a couple of days, or even weeks. It all depends on the state of mind of the dying subject and his willingness to co-operate in certain matters. Do you see?'

'No problem!' assured Aaron. 'If you'd just like to sign here, then,' (he turned the book to face Judy) 'with your name and address, and then if you could put in brackets afterwards, "professional duties", that'll cover it.'

'So sweet! Can I book some quality time with you, later?'

'No problem!'

'So very sweet! What pretty fingers you have! Are the nails your own?'

'I'm all intact!'

'Heh, heh! A sense of humour, too! And those devilish blue eyes? They're not coloured contact lenses?'

'I'm one hundred per cent the real thing!'

'Sweet as a nut! Now you'd better show me to my room so I can wash up and get changed.'

Aaron took Judy Garbo to the Pastoral Suite, so called because its large window (it took up almost an entire wall) looked out over a green field, where sheep and cows grazed and chickens fussed in the shade of large trees. Beyond this area of vivid green, where sprinklers constantly played and a small stream wound, was the desert. The contrast between green fecundity and desert aridity was nowhere more marked at the palace than here. One moment you might be gazing at a quiet scene in a New England springtime, the next you were firmly aware that this was the heart of one of the dryest deserts in the world.

'Oh, it's charming!' gushed Judy, kicking off his shoes and shuffling to the window. 'The most cynical man would find peace here. Do you get many requests for funerals? - I mean, I've only just discovered the place but already I'm thinking I'd love to be buried here.'

'Oh, all the time.'

'I bet!' Judy threw his hat and coat onto the bed. He was wearing a sky-blue suit, black shirt and yellow tie, and it was apparent that his long golden curly hair was a wig. The make-up on his face was gravely overdone.

'The graveyard is by the nondenominational chapel at the back just outside the palace walls,' Aaron continued. 'It's very peaceful. Our funeral service is expensive, though - we start at fifteen thousand dollars. Alternatively, you can simply choose to have your ashes scattered here. That's a lot cheaper - a thousand dollars only.'

'I bet you've got an absolute Vesuvius of ash at the palace.'

'It is a popular service.'

'I do think it's important to have one's final resting place in a good atmosphere; and, oh, I just feel so much good magic around me right now!'

The room was simply furnished with the usual comfortable bedroom fittings, including a fridge well stocked with drinks and snacks. Aaron pointed out a loose-leafed portfolio that lay on the desk:

'That's a catalogue of all our services. You'll find a list of all the things we offer in there. There are photographs and descriptions of all

Paradise Palace

the boys, a map of the palace, the phone number of our switchboard - the telephone is by the bed - the number of the phone sex line. You can order meals in your room, of course. Or have them down in either of our two restaurants. You'll also find descriptions of the excursions and games we offer and how to enrol in them.'

'My!'

'Um. Anything else you need to know?'

'No, I think that wraps up about everything. Except for, well…' He gave a little cough and his teeth shot neatly out into the palm of his hand. He placed them on the desk, then sank to his knees: not without some creaking awkwardness - gradually, as he revealed more of himself, Aaron was having to adjust his impression of his age sharply upwards. At first, he had thought him possibly mid thirties. Now, he seemed more mid sixties. But age, experience and a toothless mouth sharpen skill, and he gave a good blow-job. Soon Aaron was whimpering uncontrollably, the sweat running down his contorted face and smooth chest. And when Judy inserted expert fingers into his sphincter he could no longer hold himself back. He came violently, splashing cum over Judy's mouth and down the front of his suit.

Moments later, Judy was wiping himself down as if nothing happened - Aaron was always amazed at how quickly most of the men made the transition between the extreme of sexual passion to the business of everyday affairs - and saying, 'Now, I'll need a couple of hours to shower and have a little nap. Could you send someone up with a little bite to eat and a lemonade at about, say, four o'clock? And then I'll try and fix up a meeting with Mr Jed Howitzer.'

'No problem!'

'Oh, you're so sweet! And so much cum! You could fertilise the whole of the Nile delta if the Egyptian government ever got into difficulties.'

'I do my best!'

'Heh, heh! Cutie! Now run along and let's get on with the story.'

Peter Slater

Chapter Eleven

Toby awoke, stretching like a kitten into easeful consciousness. My, that had been a sweet sleep! His eyes took in the time on his bedside clock. Oh, gosh, he had been out for hours! And then he noticed the winking light on his answering machine, and remembered his two summonses. He played the tape again and found yet another two calls from Washington stressing the urgency of Sam's request.

Mumbling, 'A boy's work is never done,' he slipped gracefully out of bed.

Evenings could sometimes get a little chilly out in the desert, so quite a few of the boys chose to dress at this time. Most of the guests appreciated the contrast: a well-dressed boy can be one of the delights of the universe. Responding to the serious-sounding nature of the telephone requests, Toby took a rather sober suit from his wardrobe. He prepared himself carefully and slowly for the evening ahead. Sitting at his dressing table in a pair of Calvin Kleins, he applied the lightest touches of mascara to his eyelashes and brows, and barely noticeable dabs of powder to his cheeks. Next, a little light perfume. A ring in his left ear. Then he stood up, put on a white cotton shirt and socks. Grey trousers and Gucci shoes. A tie from Liberty's of London, patterned with alphabet letters. And, finally, his Misumake jacket.

'Ready, Toby?' he said to himself. 'Just about, dear. Don't forget to brush your hair!'

Oh, reflected in the full-length mirror, trying to set an old-fashioned parting into his hair, he looked good enough to eat! There. Now he was ready. Look out, Wall Street!

A nervous boy knocks softly at the door of room 33, the chief's room, otherwise known as Valhalla, home of the gods. He swallows and straightens his tie and remembers how it was when he had come here for the first time for his first interview. He had not long stayed clothed in his suit, back then. The boy's cock swells again and his hand idly strokes his crotch.

Receiving no answer, Toby knocked again, a little louder. He really should have responded to the chief's request straight away. Sam Greatorix was kindness itself, but he could not tolerate laxness. Toby took a deep breath and licked his lips.

'Idiot,' he murmured to himself.

The door opened and Washington ushered him into the room where Sam lay sleeping.

'What took ya so long, fella?' asked Washington. 'And don't say you were with Frank Grunwitz, because I saw him in the pool downstairs a couple hours ago.'

'I needed to sleep, was all,' said Toby, defensively.

'Ya needed ta sleep!' Washington echoed with derision. 'Well, let me tell you, fella, it's been hell over here. The chief tried to take his own life.'

'What?'

'You heard right. He's been going through some kinda crisis - obviously, something about which we know nothing. I dunno, money problems, maybe. Tax? I dunno. I've been talking to some of the other boys and there's a rumour some wife has got a million dollar lawsuit on him for turning her husband into a homosexual. I dunno what it is. You know what he's like, he won't confide in any of us. But he's been asking - frantically, baby - for you. He trusts you, Toby, far more than he ever did any of us.'

'I can't advise him on lawsuits brought by frustrated dykes!' protested Toby.

'No, but you can listen, Toby, sweetheart. You're the father-confessor, around here. People feel they can pour out their whole souls to you, and you'll only listen and not be judgemental.'

'Don't we all do that?'

'No way, sweetie! If anyone starts on me telling me about their cruel parents and their relationship with their pet monkeys, I tell 'em to go and talk it all over with you. That's what we all do around here. Didn't you know? You get all the referrals. We call you "The Priest". Didn't ya know?'

Toby shook his head, truly astonished.

'I thought… Well, I thought I got a lot of clients who didn't want sex so much as a long talk - but I thought that was how it was with all you guys. Oh, gee! Oh, gee! The things you learn!'

'Anyway, shmanyway, that's how it is. But the thing is, right now I don't think the chief is about to wake up for a good while. Doctor Max has just given him another huge sedative - the kind they use to stun bull elephants in the Serengeti, apparently - so nothing's gonna wake him for quite some hours. Do you want to stay?'

'Hey, look, I will. But not right now. I just have one other appointment that I have to go to. If, like you say, the chief won't wake for hours, it won't matter if I just pop away for, I don't know, an hour? Will it?'

'Up to you, fella.'

'Look, I'll be as quick as I can, but there's really no point my being here when he's like this. I'll just get my other business sorted out and I'll come straight back. I promise. Relieve you of your shift. I'll be here when he wakes up.'

'Okay. But make sure you are. This is serious, Toby. Honestly, I've never seen the chief in this sort of state before. He's got a confession to make.'

'I'll be right back. Promise. And, hey, Washington, give us a kiss to send me on my way!'

The naked black boy and the besuited white entwined in a passionate embrace.

It was extremely unfortunate that, bull elephants notwithstanding, Sam Greatorix should awaken again no more than five minutes after Toby had left.

'Is he here, yet?'
'Aw, gee, chief, he was here but a few minutes ago!'
'Could he not watch one hour?'
'Sorry, chief?'
'He couldn't wait.'

Paradise Palace

'He's coming back. He saw you were sleeping and…'

'It's all over…' With difficulty he hauled himself into a sitting position and signalled that Washington should come closer. 'Listen,' he said. 'When - if - Toby deigns to return, this is what I want you to do…' He whispered some words into Washington's ear.

'You sure, chief? I mean…'

'I'm sure. That's what I want. Do it.'

Before Washington could question further, Sam Greatorix fell back into sleep.

'In!' came a faint voice in response to Toby's knock on Wendell's door.

Toby entered. Used to strange sights, he was not as surprised as he might have been at the scene that met his eyes. The black dwarf was naked and suspended horizontally from the ceiling by a device of ropes and pulleys. His remarkable penis hung straight down like a length of rubber hose pipe. Another man, dressed in a rubber diving suit, was pelting him with tomatoes.

'My, my!' greeted Wendell. 'Lookee how you're dressed! Have you got an invite to Madame de Pompadour's wedding? The things you see! The things you see! You ever seen anyone as hung as me, Toby? Kinda makes ya jealous, don't it? Built like a pony, hung like a horse!'

Toby laughed kindly: he was that kind of boy.

'This dick has been my admission key to some of the highest establishment buildings in the land! Jed! You can stop throwing those tomatoes, now! Yes, sirree! The Pentagon, the Oval Office. I've walked in the White House rose garden with Eleanor Roosevelt - but you're too young ever to have heard of her. One of her closest associates was a very good friend of mine… a real good friend…' He appeared to go momentarily into some kind of trance.

Toby nodded. He stood, hands clasped in front of his stomach like a dentist preparatory to making an assault on the teeth of a nervous patient. He wished that he were not wearing the suit. If Wendell wanted him for dirty play it would invariably get messy and the one thing the palace lacked was a dry cleaning facility.

Peter Slater

'How'd ya like ten thousand dollars, boy?' Wendell asked suddenly.

'Er, we're not allowed to accept tips, sir. Within reason and our own individual limits, we're happy to go along with whatever you guests would like us to do.'

'I'm truly pleased to hear that; but I don't want you to do anything. Toby, I want ya to leave this place.'

'I'm sorry, sir?'

'You heard right. I want ya to leave, and I'll give ya ten thousand dollars to do it.'

'I'm sorry, I can't do that right now.'

'You're worried about future income. Ten thousand dollars and a contract to appear in my next two movies. How about it?'

'I'm sorry, but I can't.'

'I'm not offering enough, am I? How much do you earn here?'

Toby was under binding contract not to reveal that amount, but suffice it to say that before the end of the year he would have earned many times more than the ten thousand dollars Wendell was offering.

'Oh, sure, I respect that you can't tell me that,' Wendell continued. 'But I tell ya what. Write down a figure on a slip of paper - any figure - and I'll let you have it if you agree to my request.'

'Why do you want me to leave?'

'You're too innocent, and that sense of your innocence is interfering with my pleasure at being here.'

'I'm hardly innocent, sir, I…'

'Yeah, well, innocence can be a matter of interpretation. Look, kid, thirty thousand dollars and starring rights in my next three major movies. What ya say? And I shouldn't have to point out that many of my major stars in the past have gone onto lucrative advertising work with Levi Strauss, Calvin Klein, Coca Cola… I'm offering you your future on a plate, Toby. A chance to break free of this place. You won't be able to remain here forever, ya know. You boys have got a sell-by date stamped on all your pretty butts. Think of the future!'

'Take the offer, kid!' urged Jed.

Paradise Palace

'It's security,' reminded Wendell. 'There's no security in a place like this.'

'I'm sorry, sir, but I'm obliged under contract to stay at the Paradise Palace for at least a further year and...'

'Contract! Contracts are made to be broken!'

'And, besides,' Toby continued bravely, 'it's not just a matter of contract. I feel - we all feel, here - that Sam's a personal friend and we none of us want to let him down. He's a good man.'

'A good man,' Wendell echoed softly. 'A good man.' Up till now he had appeared to be rising towards anger, but now his attitude softened and he quieted. 'You're right, fella. Sam Greatorix is one of the best men that ever walked the face of this goddamn earth. Consider my offer, kid. That's all I can say. Go away and think about it. Can ya promise me that?'

'Sure,' said Toby.

'Good kid. Okay, you can go.'

Toby hesitated a moment. Then, 'Go! ya hear?' Wendell barked, at last giving vent to pent-up aggression.

After the boy was gone, Wendell and Jed remained frozen as two waxworks. Indeed, someone passing the window might have thought them lifeless, but for a steady drip of tears from Wendell's eyes. Finally, Wendell spoke: 'No more tomatoes, today, Jed. No more tomatoes.'

When Toby returned to Sam's - and he did so promptly - he was seized by rough hands before he had a chance to knock on the door.

'Hey, what's up, fellas? What's the matter?'

His two masked assailants - from the team of security guards that Sam employed, more because he loved the uniforms of the New York Police Department than for any pressing need to maintain law and order - told him to keep quiet and not struggle and he would come to no harm.

'What is this? I need to speak to Sam! What have I done?'

'We're acting on orders.'

'Orders? I...'

His hands were twisted behind his back and clamped into handcuffs.

'Aw, gee! I just don't believe this! Look, I don't mind playing a game for someone... Is this someone's game? Honestly, I don't mind, and I'll do it later. But I've got an urgent appointment with Sam right now. Let me go, and I'll go along with you later. Handcuffs and uniforms - I can buy into that. Who's put you up to this? Mr Liebowitz? Just tell me. I like ta know. I have a right to know. And I'll go along with it. Right along with it. But later. Who's it for?'

'These are Sam's orders.'

'Sam's orders? I don't get it. He's in no state to play this kind of game - and it's not like him, anyway. Sam Greatorix? The chief?'

'Sam Greatorix. You're under house arrest, Toby. Please don't struggle.'

Sensing the hopelessness of his position, Toby relaxed. He was taken, by hidden back staircases and dark passages, to the basement of the palace. And there, in the very cellars, he was thrown - yes, thrown, these guards were brutes - into a small cell. He lay on the floor and looked around him. A single bed, a carpet, a table and chair and one high, barred window. That was all he had. The door clanged shut. He sat on the carpet, pulled up his knees and buried his face in his hands. What had he done?

Paradise Palace

Chapter Twelve

When Judy Garbo was fully rested, he got on the phone to the palace switchboard and was connected with Jed Howitzer.

'I'm surprised you weren't at the gates to meet me,' said Judy in his characteristic furred Southern whisper.

'I didn't know when to expect you,' apologised Jed.

'Oh, come now, honey! I clattered in with as much silence as a blue whale's orgasm.'

'I'm sorry, I was tied up with Wendell Banks - remember him?'

'You still working for that shit?'

'Don't call him that - he's not a bad man.'

'You wouldn't say that if you knew how many people have come to me wanting to sue him for defamation of character. But you wouldn't know about that, because not one case ever gets to court - Wendell Banks always offers a substantial out-of-court settlement. A sure proof of guilt and a sure way of denying me my full fee.'

'Well, like you say, I don't know anything about that and I'm not sure I want to know. He's my boss, and I'll stick by him.'

'Highly commendable. But let's not fall out over your lapses in good taste. I came to give you a little legal advice. A matter of changing a will?'

'That's right.'

'Is this phone line secure?'

'I don't know. Like you, I'm only a guest here. Why don't you come to my room? We can have a little discussion and then go on and meet my new friend.'

'Sure thing! Whereabouts are you?'

Jed supplied Judy with the necessary details and, ten minutes later, Judy, a briefcase in one hand, a map of the palace in the other, was on his way. This time, he had dropped the semi-drag, was dressed in a suit and tie and wore a less extravagant make-up.

'The situation is this…'

Peter Slater

They were in Jed's room, sitting in two armchairs before a window which overlooked a swimming pool. Judy was sipping a long dry Martini and Jed was speaking:

'... It's a guy called Russ Schlagfarn. Heard of him?'

'Are we talking the oil and cattle baron who started back in the depression with a single can of machine oil and an emaciated calf?'

'That's the guy!'

'I hate these rags-to-riches stories, they're all so false. You'd know that if you'd been in courtrooms as long as I have. You get all the truth in those places, believe me - even if the guilty only rarely get convicted. Truth is no weapon in court. I know all about old Schlagfart. One thing his biographers failed, somehow inexplicably, to mention was the fact that his father just happened to find an oil well on the family farm. That's how Schlagfart Enterprises Inc. got started - nothing to do with the teenage Russ selling his calf at a profit and oiling some guy's car so well that he got offered a job in a garage. If the teenage Russ ever oiled some guy's anything, it wasn't going to be his car. But, anyway, who cares how he came by his money, so long as it doesn't all go to his equally vile relations! What d'ya say?'

'That's why I asked you to come,' said Jed.

'What's the score? - and who's that cutie by the pool with a face that would melt butter, and balls any bull would be proud of?'

'Who? Him? The dark one? I dunno, sorry. Like I say, I'm not long here myself. Me and Wendell, we've come here to do a movie based on Shakespeare's Tempest, and...'

'Okay, okay! I asked who the boy was, not "Will you tell me your whole life history starting at your mother's breast?" Is there a will already?'

'Yep.'

'So it's a matter of changing it. Is the will here?'

'He's had a copy faxed.'

'Good. Has that boy got an erection starting? I'd say he has! That's how I like to see boys - just at that first moment of stirring! Now, stop making me digress! Where is this fax?'

Paradise Palace

Jed had it to hand and gave it to Judy. It was a three-page document, and he read it carefully.

'It's complex,' Judy said at length. 'All trust funds and whatnot. Has he said what he wants to leave you?'

'The whole lot.'

'His entire fortune? Well, that's simple. We just write a whole new will. But I don't recommend it. The family'll fight it tooth and nail, and the case'll drag through the courts for twenty years, by which time there'll be no money left - the lawyers will have had it all. Better by far is to try to persuade him to leave you a nice little sum in the form of a subsidiary bequest, a codicil at the end. Oh, god!' he sighed, as the boy he'd been looking at began to make love with another, by the side of the pool. 'This every day! How does anybody ever get any work done?'

'They don't - this is a holiday centre.'

'Aren't you the little wiseacre? Such pert buttocks that boy's got! Doesn't it make you yearn to be young again? Once your eighteen candles have been lit and blown out on the cake you never again get those firm, everlasting erections - you know, the ones that orgasms never seem to diminish. Do they ever have clingfilm parties here?'

'How much is "a nice little sum"?' Jed was keen to return to the matter in hand. 'I mean, how much could I ask for without the family challenging me?'

'Oh, I don't know!' Judy was exasperated by the interruption to his fantasy. 'Ten million? How much do you want?'

'Ten million! But, lookee, he offered me everything - the guy's practically a billionaire!'

'I've already explained, honey-bunny, why you can't expect that. Get real! And if the old boy agrees to this codicil in a straightforward manner, that's a better deal than most of his other beneficiaries are getting. I mean, lookee here at his poor grandson who has to agree to a year spent being homeless in the Bowery before he can access the money put aside for him in a trust fund. And his wife has to take a full-page spread in The New York Times admitting to the fact that she was possessed by demons when she attended a Republican fund-raising dinner in support of George Bush back in 1992. In the light of all that, an unconditional ten million dollars seems a miracle! Believe me, try for any more and you won't get it. I've spent my life in this business. Take my word for it. Go for the simple ten.'

'Actually, it's not so simple. He has mentioned a certain condition.'

'And what's that?'

'He wants one last orgasm.'

'What?'

'One last cum, before witnesses, and he's said I can have whatever I want. "Draw up whatever you like and after that I'll sign," he told me.'

'Is that going to be a problem?'

'He's eighty-eight.'

'Ah!'

'And has been staying here for the past three months without any sexual adventures, so far as I can make out. And since I've been here, I've not been able to stir anything. He spends all his time propped up in bed, watching Bugs Bunny videos.'

'Is he sane?'

'Oh, sure! That's not a problem. I like Bugs Bunny.'

'So do I. But I haven't developed a fetish for him. And what about life expectancy? How much time does he have for this one last big one? A man of eighty-eight can live on for another decade.'

'Doctor Max - he's the house physician - gives him another few weeks, at the most. It's a degenerative heart condition.'

'So let's get this clear. He agrees to putting you in his will, but he'll only sign this agreement after he's had the orgasm?'

'That's it.'

'Look, much as I hate to draw myself away from this window, I think we'd better go and make a visit to Mr Russ Schlagfart.'

Receiving no answer to his insistent knocking, Jed decided it would be all right to use the key Mr Schlagfarn had given him.

Paradise Palace

'He told me to use it anytime I didn't get an answer,' he explained, 'He has this dread of dying and not being found for months. Not that that could ever happen here - the chamberboys all have pass keys and clean every room every day and leave fresh flowers and so forth. MR SCHLAGFARN! IT'S JED! Okay, let's go in.'

The first thing Judy noticed on entering was the icy cold. Mr Schlagfarn - a true Texan - loathed heat and kept the air-conditioning going on mega-drive. The second thing he saw was horrifying and he gave an involuntary yelp, the quick final bleat of a rabbit caught in the jaws of a wicked fox. Mr Schlagfarn was lying naked on his bed, his mouth gaping open and eyes staring at the ceiling.

'Nyerrrrr! What's up, doc!' came from the massive television screen set in the wall opposite the bed.

'He's dead!' Judy spoke in the whisper that is customary in the presence of new corpses - as if the recently-dead possessed exceptional qualities of hearing and could not bear loud noise.

'Naw, he's okay,' said Jed. 'Just asleep. He's had so many facelifts, the skin's so tight that he can't close his eyes any more. He's breathing, see?'

For all his great age, Mr Schlagfarn kept a decent body and, at a closer look, Judy saw that his well-formed chest was indeed rising and falling.

'RUSS! RUSS, BABY!' Jed shouted, giving the old man a hearty shake.

Watching closely, Judy witnessed a remarkable sight. The old man's green eyes changed from non-seeing to seeing - you could tell straight away; but what different form the eyes took was impossible to describe. Perhaps the colour deepened, perhaps the muscles contracted; perhaps, perhaps: the process was one of the mysteries of life.

'Here I am!' greeted Russ. 'Where's the wabbit?'

Judy gave Jed a worried look. He had seen many a disputed will case lost by reason of insanity.

'The wabbit's on the wall,' said Jed.

Peter Slater

Russ smiled, then he turned his head, saw Judy and demanded in darker tones, 'Who's this punk?'

'That's my solicitor, Judy Garbo.'

'She's the butchest dyke I ever saw. Are you charging an entrance fee for dykes to come and view my naked body? See what they've been missing all these years.'

'I'm a man,' said Judy. 'But I'm certainly envious of your fine body.'

'Pah!' Russ Schlagfarn wasn't one to be flattered by fine words. 'The hydraulics have broken down - as I'm sure Jed has already told you - so "fine" doesn't come into it.'

'You're a good age.'

'I'm a goddamn awful age. Listen, mister, no lawyer has ever yet benefited from me, so you can cut all the soft soap crap. You know the score. I'm head over heels in love with young Jed, here, and if he can get me to cum one last time, he inherits my entire fortune. Draw up the papers!'

You are one crazy cookie! thought Judy. Nevertheless, he said, 'Certainly! I think first of all, though, we need to have a little discussion, to sort out practicalities...'

Chapter Thirteen

The guard was gentle, but insistent: Toby was to remove all his clothes and consent to having his hands tied behind his back.

'I'm sorry, son, but that's how it is. This order comes with the highest authority - well, you know we wouldn't dare do this to you without that authority.'

'But what else does he say?' asked Toby, unbuttoning his flies and tugging down his trousers. 'I mean, I don't mind being naked - I feel pretty strange wearing clothes around here, anyway - but I don't get it with the handcuffs bit.'

'Between you and me, son, the word is that Sam is expecting an extra-special guest and he wants you to be ready. That means that he doesn't want you to run the risk of picking up anything in the meantime from any of the other guests - hence your quarantine. And he wants you in a state of high sexual desperation - hence the handcuffs to stop you jerking off. That's what I heard, anyways.'

This was the story that the insanely-jealous Sam wanted Toby to believe. In truth, Toby was imprisoned because Sam couldn't bear the idea of another man having sex with him.

'Well, why couldn't he have kept me under house arrest in my room and supplied a pair of boxing gloves?'

'I can't answer all the intricate details, son, all I know is, well, I just need...'

Toby was now down to just his Calvin Kleins, and the guard slipped his hand inside, pulled out the boy's cock and began to massage it between thumb and three fingers. As the welcome sexual charge took hold of him, Toby groaned, leant forward to rest against the guard and licked his lips. 'Please!' he whispered.

'Take it easy, son. We'll help you through with this.'

He eased Toby's briefs further down and took a firmer hold of his cock. Then came the sound of running.

'You're gonna haveta be quick, son. C'mon, baby! Fuckin' shoot.'

Peter Slater

They kissed passionately and the guard's hand pumped tighter and faster...

But to no avail.

In moments, the rest of the security team was upon them and pulling them apart.

'Break it up, you guys! Break it up!'

Sam, watching on a video link from his sick bed, nodded sad approval as the guard was taken away and the boy Toby, finally made naked and handcuffed, crawled back into his cell and lay down on the crude bed.

'No-one shall lay their filthy hands on thee,' he whispered. 'Thou art mine and only mine.'

Hours slink past. Wander around the palace. Check out what's happening. Glance in at boy on boy, boy on man. There's a sight: a boy, fair-haired and blue-eyed, lying in a long trough covered in sliced fruit: oranges, apples, papaya, melon, blackberries, cloudberries, strawberries, redcurrants, whitecurrants, blackcurrants, peaches, grapes and apricots. He's all alone, waiting for the feast to begin. Soon, it will.

Judo Garbo reads dry words to Jed and Russ, who nod sagely. Jed's mind is only half on the text; he is wondering if Doctor Max might be able to help out with a little injection of something into the old man's cock.

Wendell remains hanging from the ceiling. He has been there for hours and he will remain for hours. Jed should have returned by now to help him down; but what the heck: this was love, and in love, as in life, it was a matter of no pain, no gain. Belief, dearies, is all.

Where's Sam?

Sam sat in his great throne seat - a gorgeously-decorated affair with a high back, ornamented with twisting snakes and lions' heads, and boasting a red velvet cushion and armrests in the shapes of lions' paws - and regarded the video screen which still featured his captive darling. (Who was expecting him to be watching Russ Schlagfarn's Bugs Bunny

Paradise Palace

tapes? Pay attention readers, and hold this book in both hands.)

Sam wore a white silk robe, richly embroidered with colourful birds, fruits and forests, white leggings and doveskin slippers. These last rare items were manufactured personally for Sam Greatorix, according to an ancient Persian technique, by the leading Persian slipper maker in Isfahan.

He propped his cheek against a left hand smothered with rings of diamond, jet and ruby. The jet struck an uncomfortably sombre note: life is not all hilarity. And Sam watched, and he growled, and he pondered the mystery of love. Why should we so desire one person above all others, so that every other sexual opportunity seems vile and worthless? Why do we hate the very thought of our loved one mating with another? This last concern was uppermost in Sam's fevered mind. Here was one of his boys, in his brothel, and he, Sam, could not bear the thought of him carrying out the work which he was paying him for.

But the situation was more complex than simple love and its usual pains. We all know about jealousy - and it can be founded on sound reason. Our loved one may find another lover more sexually satisfying; therefore, it makes sense to seek to deny him the opportunity of sexual exploration. That much is clear and reasonable. However, Sam had departed somewhat from reason. Love's madness.

Think about it. If Sam wanted, he could quite easily reserve Toby exclusively for himself. He could make him his pet, his Prince, and simply insist that no other should sleep with him on pain of expulsion from the palace. Of course he could do that. No problem. But that would be to deny himself something: one of the sweetest (perhaps bittersweet would be more accurate), most curious pleasures of human existence: the dear ache of longing. Sehnsucht, the Germans call it (cf. Schubert, Goethe, Thomas Mann, et al.). Perhaps we forget how lovely it is to regard someone from afar, and yearn. The boy we see everyday at the local garage - sometimes leaning over to clean a car, so that his grimy tee-shirt rises briefly to reveal two inches of skin; the boy in the skin-tight jeans who always catches the same subway train as you each morning - once, just once, you brushed against him: sacred memory. The waiter at the local deli with those to-die-for green eyes. These boys are forever new, they are reborn with every passing glance, and they can have skin that tastes just as you like in your imagination, and cocks, huge or modest, just as you like, and sexual preferences just as you like. They are forever perfect: in your fantasies, their movements have the smooth perfection of water, there is no awkwardness. Their breath is sweet as almonds and their teeth white as Arctic ice.

Once you sleep with a boy, something is forever lost. The sexual act is never quite as perfect as it might be, a little wince of unwelcome pain here, a small disappointment there. Yearning is forever perfect, one's fantasies will only permit what gives pleasure.

Sam Greatorix, after years of fulfilled desire and requited love, now yearned for the necessary opposite. Compare it to food. If you have regular meals and good food and never go without, you lack that chief ingredient: a healthy appetite. You might enjoy your food and go to great pains to prepare it or have it prepared for you; but it never tastes so good as when you are ravenously hungry. And the same with thirst. A long, cold drink to quench a dry body: what could be finer? An endless supply of drink can never be the same.

So Sam regarded Toby; and he yearned.

Knowing, however, that this emotional complexity could not possibly be understood at the Paradise Palace (and also fearing that this was an emotional weakness that might somehow diminish him in the sight of his boys), he had word put out that Toby was to be reserved for a wealthy Middle Eastern Sheikh who was now on his way from Damascus, travelling by land and sea in order that the boy should have as long as possible to remain sexually pure.

Sam watched the video screen. His physiognomy was that of a monstrous dictator plotting some new nefarious scheme in order to increase the extent of his power. He breathed, and he watched. He was glad that he had locked Toby in a cell rather than allowing him to remain under house-arrest in his room. If the boy for whom one yearns is suffering in some way, then it is a potent fantasy to imagine oneself

Paradise Palace

rescuing him. Sam would one day rescue Toby. Perhaps.

All news spread quickly at the palace, and not a few clients went either personally to complain about the disappearance of Toby to the boys at reception or rang up Curt on the switchboard. Curt had to talk one man out of a suicide bid, and persuade another that if he stayed on at the palace for the full duration of his holiday, he would - honestly - find other boys as lovely as dear, departed Toby.

Wendell Banks was told the story by Jed, when the latter eventually came to release dim from his hanging. Wendell did not believe the yarn about the coming Sheikh - that was a transparent lie. Toby had been sequestrated for Sam's personal pleasure. No doubt about it. The boy's incarceration, however, gave him a diabolical idea.

'Can I trust you, Jed?'

Wendell was, by this time, neck deep in a bubble bath, smoking a cigar, Jed on a chair by his side, legs crossed, arms folded.

'All the years we've known each other, boss!'

'Sure. We've been a team, haven't we, boy? Got ourselves in a few scrapes, one way or another, and always managed to sweet talk our way out. You've saved my skin not a few times, and I've saved yours. Remember Chicago?'

Jed visibly stiffened. 'Remember Chicago,' he repeated. 'Why'd ya say that, boss? 'Course I remember. But it's better forgotten, ain't it?'

'Yeah, sure!' Wendell lifted his head back and puffed a few smoke rings. 'Forgotten!'

'You promised never to say anything to anyone... It'd be the finish of me.'

'And I always keep my word. Forget Chicago.'

'Forget Chicago.'

'Now, let's forget Chicago and change the subject entirely. I want you to help me carry out a little something. A trifle.'

'Sure, boss. Anything.'

'Murder Toby.'

'Boss?'

'You heard right. Let's dispense with the "Why, gosh, and oh, my

- 79 -

god!" dialogue. You know why I want him out. He won't be bought, so he has to be dead.'

'Isn't that a bit drastic?'

'Call it love's madness, son. Now I was thinkin' of poison.'

'I won't do it!'

'Look, I thought I said we were to do away with all that debate crap! If I asked ya to go out and buy me a doughnut, ya wouldn't give me no grief; and I want this little request to be just the same. Sometimes I ask you to do one thing, sometimes another. This is just another thing.'

'But...'

'De-daa-daa!' Wendell sang the opening notes of a Frank Sinatra song that was not 'New York! New York!'

'How, boss?'

'Well, guns, knives and strangulation are surely out - they're not practical in the circumstances, and I've always hated that sort of mortal clumsiness. It just so happens, however, that I have with me a little phial of Amanita Foscurum, which I think will do the trick. It's a little poison manufactured from mushrooms by a tribe in the Amazonian rainforest. It's completely tasteless and completely deadly. And, best of all, it leaves no trace in the body after death. Once it gets into the bloodstream, it swims along until it reaches the heart then it stretches out green fingers - as you might say - which grab the heart and hold it until it stops beating. After which, our Amanita Foscurum, following a natural chemical process of reaction with the host body, simply converts into ordinary body salts and is untraceable.'

'How about that!'

'It can be taken with food or liquid. I've always found it's best when stirred into a milkshake because then you can be certain not to leave any telltale traces on the side of a plate, or anything like that.'

'Is death painful?'

'Not at all.'

An honest man, this was the first lie Wendell had spoken in many years. In fact, death by Amanita Foscurum is exquisitely painful. The

Paradise Palace

subject grasps his chest and screams for air and life. But nothing can ever be done. The cause of death is identical to that of a massive heart attack. All those accounts you've ever read in the papers concerning people who have suffered fatal heart attacks completely out of the blue, and often at a young age - they're all cases of Amanita Foscurum poisoning. Jealous lovers, business rivals, simple hatred: that's just the way it is.

'When do you want me to do it?'

'There's no great hurry. Within the week, say. It won't be difficult. You just have to get yourself down to the kitchens and find out which tray is destined for him. I'll, er, of course, be giving you a small bonus. I don't expect you to carry out this sort of work out of love. Perhaps the figure I originally offered the boy voluntarily to leave town?'

'Thanks, boss!'

'Well, it would add a certain ironic flavour to the drama. Now. Our time here isn't all pleasure and play. We came to work and tomorrow I want to start filming - Sam Greatorix or no Sam Greatorix. You ready for that?'

'Sure, boss!'

'Okey, dokey! Well, then, help me out of this goddamn bath and we'll set to and work out a few preliminaries.'

Chapter Fourteen

Poor Jed. Everything seemed to be on his shoulders. He had to star in a Shakespeare movie, coax an old man into a final orgasm, and now murder a boy of whom he had become very fond. He liked Toby - he was the first boy Jed had made love with on arrival at the palace, and that added a certain sentimental weight to his natural affection for a kid who was so obviously sweet, honest and kind.

Jed lay in bed, alone, that night, and told himself that this time next week everything might be all over and he could ride off into the sunset a wealthy man. Heck, he would be very rich! If Russ Schlagfarn passed away - perhaps a fatal heart attack inspired by final sexual triumph - that would mean a cool few million. And there was the ten thousand dollars from Wendell, on Toby's death. All money identified with death. It was not a pleasant thought. Jed felt a little like a contract killer. Maybe he was a contract killer. Aw, no, he wasn't like that at all. He had no choice in the matter of Toby's death. He wasn't doing it for the money, he had been blackmailed.

Jed turned onto his side and curled into a foetus position. He clutched a green rag scented with Chanel No.5, the scent favoured by his long-lost mother. He thought of his Ma every day. A scene on a dust road in Mississippi: a small boy stands watching a bus as it drives away between fields of low, green corn. It disappears in a dip of a hill, appears again after a while, far distant, disappears in the gently undulating landscape, appears, disappears and is gone forever. The boy turns and buries himself in the apron of his grandmother.

April Howitzer had been proclaimed Miss Hartland County 1976 and no longer felt that her lifestyle could admit a small boy and an aged parent, who lived above a shoe shop. So she was off. Young Jed did not blame her - indeed, felt there was nothing to forgive. She had done what was right. It was his fault that she had to go away, because he was a just a kid and, of course, he was a nuisance and a hindrance. He only hoped that she might be able to spare the time to call back, some day. She never did. There was never so much as a letter. But Jed understood this, too: his mother was now a star and could not possibly have the time to write letters. Someday, though, they would be reunited; and, in the meantime, her scent kept her fresh in his memory.

They were to start shooting Act One, Scene Two (revised edition) at 11 a.m. (Act One, Scene One - the scene aboard the ship that is wrecked owing to the excesses of the onboard orgy - would have to be postponed until the set could be built.) The scene concerned the sailors' first arrival on the island and their encounter with the fairy boy slave, Ariel. The part, which was to have been played by Toby, would have to be recast, but that should not present any great difficulty. All the chosen cast members were to report to the Paradise Garden promptly. Wendell had been granted exceptional permission to film here from Sam - before Sam's decline, obviously.

A bower constructed of banana leaves and the fronds of a coconut palm, was erected beside the water-lily lake. Here, on a bed of frangipani blossom, Prospero, the slave-master of the island was making love with Ariel. Notwithstanding the fact that his sole declared passion was still only for Sam, and that he loathed boys, Prospero was played by Wendell Banks. His Ariel was Rob, twenty years old, with a tan and crew-cut. To denote his special magic status, Rob's body was marked with yellow and blue lines.

The scene concluded with the boy beggaring his master whilst singing:

> 'Come unto these yellow sands
> And then take hands
> Curtsied when you have and kissed
> The wild waves whist
> Foot it fealty here and there
> And sweet sprites bear
> The Burton. Hark, hark
> The watchdogs bark.'

Naturally, Rob had not had time to learn the lines, so he read from a script held shakily in front of him by an elderly volunteer.

'Okay, cut!' called Wendell, when Rob was spent.

'What the fuck's all that mean?' asked Rob, clutching his condom and carefully pulling out.

'It means, ignorant Yankee, "I want these shipwrecked sailors to cum on the yellow sands of this island and fuck me stoopid." Now Ariel has sung this, and the sailors can hear him, but don't know whereabouts he is. So Ferdinand - JED! where the hell are ya?'

'Here, boss!'

'Good kid. Now you step out the water-lily pond here and ask, "Where should this music be? I' Th.' air or the 'art?" Got that speech?'

'Sure, boss.'

'Good. And as soon as you've said it, you see Miranda - that's Prospero's other love-boy, Curt here - and you fall in love. But Prospero says you can only have him if you pass a series of tests. Okay. Get in the Goodman water, Jed, and make sure ya come out covered in mud and dripping weed. CAMERA! ACTION!'

Some of you readers may be true Shakespeare lovers, so we will not remain with this scene a moment longer. Look on this episode as yet another of the plenitudinous interpretations of the Bard - a very loose interpretation, maybe, but done with the best intentions. Worse things have happened; better things will happen. It's just a matter of waiting.

In his gloomy cell Toby could not distinguish day from night. The single high window was shuttered on the outside. The only source of light was a bare bulb hanging from the ceiling.

We find him sleeping, curled on his bed, head beneath the pillow. Are we watching him as Sam is watching him - on video? Or are we closer? We are closer. We can feel the damp ache in his body, the sour taste in his mouth; see inside his mind: he dreams he is lying on a couch and being fellated and buggered by Swing and Swung. His cock, which Sam also cannot see, is stiff and pulsing, and small unconscious hip thrusts help keep it that way and edge him ever closer to the realisation of a wet dream. And, as readers, we may also smell the sharp, musty warmth between the tip of his cock and the sheet of the bed; and there is the sticky trail of pre-cum.

Toby's breathing quickens. His buttocks twitch and thrust more urgently - now even Sam can see that something is happening. Still asleep he is fucking into the bed - hard, harder, harder, harder; an imperceptible pause, followed by a desolate cry.

Sam watched from his throne, and it seemed as if he was not the slightest bit interested in Toby's actions. He called up Washington on his mobile phone and gave him instructions.

Life for Toby during the period of his imprisonment was curious - a mixture of deprivation and comfort, hunger and satiety, silence and sweet music. The only constant was celibacy - never was he offered the opportunity to alter that state.

During the first two days of his captivity, he was fed only bread and water. No sound was allowed to enter the cell - apart from the distant sounds of voices and footsteps. And, as we have seen, there was no furniture that could be described as comfortable. The only people he saw were the anonymous security guards. All his questions were met with a noncommittal, 'Sorry, son, we're under orders not to answer any questions.'

Things changed on day three. Toby was in a troubled dream in which, weightless, he was attempting to make love with Keanu Reeves. There they both were, floating naked above the surface of a rocky planet, neither able to reach the other. Then into this dream came an ethereal music. It was an otherworldly sound: perhaps voices or a blend of high flutes and harps, it was impossible to say. Whatever it was, it was exquisitely beautiful. The dreaming, floating Toby knew that this music was all that mattered, everything else was impermanent and of no consequence. The music alone connected him to something other, something mysterious - perhaps divinity would be not too strong a word. Keanu looked puzzled and helpless as, suddenly, Toby's erection died and Toby himself paddled his arms to take himself further and further away. Then Keanu began to disappear: first the feet, then the legs, then his chest and arms. For a long time there remained his face and cock, until his face gradually dissolved into the blue of the sky and, finally, his cock vanished, too. Leaving only the music. This is all I want and ever need thought Toby. He began to follow the music - indeed, found that it was pulling him gently towards it. Only music.

He was getting closer and closer, the sound seemed to fill his whole being and he had to fight back the tears. Ahead of him hung a silk tapestry curtain. Behind this curtain was the answer to everything. He had only to reach it and all his questions would be answered. The greatest joy would be his. He made out the pattern of sea and stars sewn onto a red background. Of course the sea: he was a Piscean.

Nearly there!

And then, of course, he awoke. But there was not the usual disappointment on awaking from a wonderful dream. This was different because the music remained here with him. Now he could recognise it as singing. Awkwardly, he eased himself into a sitting position on the side of the bed. His handcuffed arms were causing him some pain, and he winced as jagged darts of agony streaked through his shoulders.

Toby sat and listened.

Presently, a guard came and set before him a table, spread with a white cloth. Onto the table he placed a bowl of soup and some crusty bread. Toby watched with interest, but no great hunger - the days of privation had shrunk his stomach and he had no great appetite. The guard removed his handcuffs and Toby set to.

It was fish soup, and was delicious. With the first spoonful, Toby's appetite was reawakened and he ate ravenously. When he was finished, the guard cleared away the plates and brought the next course: a grilled trout with side salad and new potatoes. Toby savoured every mouthful; and, when the guard fetched in the sweet - ice cream and blueberry pie - Toby felt that he had never known such sweet joy.

The meal over, the guard returned and cleared everything away. When he was gone, Toby lay back on the bed. The man had forgotten to replace the handcuffs and Toby's hands naturally strayed to his cock. Cradling his balls in one hand he began to masturbate with the other. The sensation after so long an abstinence was extraordinary. It seemed the nerves in every corner of his body came alive. He licked the palm of his right hand and stroked it over the tip of his cock, down and under the balls and then, resuming a tight grip on the shaft, he simply masturbated vigorously. He had no need of fantasy, but his mind nevertheless supplied him the image of him fucking Keanu Reeves whilst the latter was spread-eagled over a vaulting horse.

And Sam watched - intent, but seemingly unmoved, even when Toby ejaculated in a series of vigorous spurts which fountained high and wide, splashing his face and chest, landing in his open, begging mouth and on his beseeching, warm tongue. Toby rubbed his cum into his skin and licked his fingers lovingly.

Chapter Fifteen

'Hey, Miranda, that's a real cute dick you got there! I'd love to clamp my teeth round it.'

'CUT!' roared Wendell. 'Jed, baby, where the fuck are those lines in the whole of Shakespeare?'

They were by the pond from which Jed had just emerged, naked, dripping water, covered in slime and with a strand of weed draped over his shoulder. Miranda, played by Curt, was sitting cross-legged on a Persian carpet. He wore only a black silk shirt and a thin silver necklace. Wendell was in his director's chair, his feet dangling six inches from the ground. He wore a blue silk kimono and held a megaphone in one hand, a script in the other. From time to time a boy, crouching beside him, offered him a drag on a long cigar.

Wendell, looking peeved, said, 'I thought you said we had to improvise?'

'Sure - but only in the spirit of the original. What ya done with the script me and Sam put together?'

'I lost it, boss.'

'Get him a goddamn script, someone! Jeez, Jed - you're my star. I was expecting better. You're letting down the whole show here.'

'I've never had to deal with a speaking script before, boss. It's all been, well, you know, choreography.'

'That's obvious. Here, yeah, Rob give him yours... Right. Take it from the top. No, Jed, honey, don't go back in the water. We've already got that shot. Just read your first line. Okay. We're waiting.'

Jed self-consciously tugged his cock before speaking, 'Miranda, thou art lovelier and more fair than...'

'CUT! Jed, honey-bunny, you're speaking as if you're chewing a plank of wood. Can't you feel the poetry? You're supposed to be an actor. And, anyway, those aren't your first lines. What happened to "Where should this music be? i' th' air or the 'arth?"

'I don't know what an "arth" is, boss. Aw, look, I'm a porn star,

Paradise Palace

boss, not Marlon Brando.'

'Okay, okay. Look, how about we dispose with your lines there. In fact we could cut out your lines altogether. Just look at Curt here and smoulder. Okay. Act One, Scene Two, Take Three!'

Jed could certainly play this part. He looked down at the sweet boy in his black shirt and his face was full of sexual ache. His gently massaged cock half-rose accordingly.

'Excellent!' murmured Wendell. 'CUT! Okay, good.' He slid off the chair and interposed himself between the boys. 'Now this is where I break you up.

'"Away, thou servile sea-dog. Thou canst not fuck my boy, he is mine alone..." Right, you miss out your lines there. Just smoulder some more. Jab me with your cock like it's a weapon. Great. Okay, I go on: "But perhaps it wouldst amuse me to relent and see thou perform some labours in return for sexual favour. Acquit thyself well of these deeds, and my boy Miranda shall be thine. Fail, and thou become'st part of my harem, to be used for my pleasure alone, and never shalt thou fuck young Miranda. Art thou prepared? What say'st thou?" We'll cut that bit. CUT! You don't say anything. We might have to have an earlier scene where your tongue's cut out by a gang of gay pirates into heavy SM. Camera on Jed's face. Jed, you nod slowly. Take Four! Five seconds. CUT! And let's get a shot of this cock. Take Five! ... Okey, dokey! CUT! Now we'll just do my speech and we'll intersperse shots of you, Jed, having a jerk-off, later... Take Six!

'"Ferdinand, willst thou do anything in order to gain fair Miranda? Good. Seven labours will I give thee. Each one accomplished will bring thee a step nearer to thy desired goal. The first will commence straightway. My fairies will seize thee, smother thy body in honey, tie you to a post and leave thee to the mercy of wasps and flies. For a full day thou must endure this torture. Art thou up for it? Good. Seize him fairies!" CUT!'

Accordingly, Jed was bound with ropes smeared with honey and tied to a cedar tree. At first it was easy; but then, sure enough, every bug in the State scented him out and along they came: wasps and flies,

– 89 –

of course; but also mosquitoes, ants, butterflies and beetles. Delightful tickling turned to unbearable itching and ferocious biting. Jed cried out in pain and his face bore the look of a Sebastian being martyred.

'Nearly! Nearly!' muttered Wendell as, Andy Warhol-like, he shot hour upon hour of film.

'Do we have to go on so long, boss?' asked Jed, after the second hour.

'Yep! If I have to shoot five hours for five minutes of perfect film, I'll do it. Don't worry, I'll know just when I've captured the right expression on your face. You haven't got quite the right degree of agony yet. Ya know, if you could act, I probably could get the whole thing done in ten minutes. But you can't act, so we have to wait until the real thing comes along. Boys, we could use some more honey on his balls right here - these green ants, they're really going for it!'

After the third hour, Wendell said, 'Jed you're looking too relaxed! We need agony here. We'll go on all day and all night if we don't get it. Boys - put some honey up his ass.'

When the ants began to crawl, tickling and biting, into his crack, then Jed knew what real discomfort was. He broke out into a sweat and, at last, his face contorted into exactly the right expression. He touched reality.

'That's it!' enthused Wendell. 'At last! Hold it there just a moment or two longer, Jed honey! Bewt! - as they say in Melbourne after they've buggered a coupla kangaroos. Perfect! Okey, dokey! C-UT! Untie the fella, boys!'

Once free, Jed ran headlong into the swimming pool.

Filming was completed for that day.

It took Jed a couple of days to recover from the ordeal. He lay on his bed in a darkened room, a shade over his eyes. Doctor Max prescribed calamine lotion and antihistamine tablets. Various boys took turns to rub in the calamine, and if they happened to rub it on his dick a little more vigorously than was medically necessary it was only out of a natural curiosity to witness the engorging of a member that was ten

Paradise Palace

inches when flaccid and looked to be a full ruler's length when finally erect. The balls of this incapacitated stud were also fascinating: they hung as low as those of a Friesian bull, like a couple of potatoes in a Mediaeval money pouch.

On the third day, Jed's strength returned.

As shooting was about to begin on his second labour, he had an idea which he put to Wendell. The old man listened and nodded.

If it met with his approval, their work would be seen by Russ Schlagfarn: it might fuel a fantasy and help towards his great aim of a last orgasm.

As it turned out, Mr Schlagfarn had no objection and, accordingly, Judy Garbo, who had booked in for the duration (ready to perform as an independent witness, should the need arise), wheeled him onto the set in a chair fitted with a parasol.

'If ya get the horn any time, just signal and I'll come on over and help you out,' promised Jed.

'You're a sweet boy,' said Russ and, raising a liver-spotted hand, pulled Jed closer and gave him a lingering kiss on the lips.

'There!' said Jed, kindly, 'Feel any better?'

'Much, much worse, thank you. This may be my last day.'

'Hey!' In an unseemly panic, Jed made a grope for the old boy's cock, only to be pushed away savagely.

'Leave me alone! I can't be turned on like some wretched machine. I'm flesh and blood. Go and do your acting.'

The second labour of Ferdinand was similar in some respects to the first. Whether it proved a worse agony than the first must remain a matter for conjecture and personal taste. Suffice it to say that Jed found it worse - although its after effects were not nearly so bad.

Again Jed was tied up and again smeared with honey. This time, however, he was lashed to the outside of a metal cage, his legs wide apart to allow easier access to his arse and back. And the wasps and diverse other flying and crawling insects were kept at bay by the volunteer film crew - they were not needed. Instead, his body was licked bitten and nibbled by a seemingly endless succession of boys.

Peter Slater

Their brief was to apply tongues, lips and teeth to every part of his anatomy bar his cock.

To be tantalised in this way for a short time might be fun. What torture could be more exquisite than to have a fair boy lightly lick and nibble your balls, whilst a dark boy pierced his tongue deep into your arse? And then those boys would fall away and begin masturbating within your sight whilst another pair would work on you with a dildo. Sheer joy, perhaps: and Jed's cock showed it. Erect as a drag drum majorette's baton, it throbbed and swayed and silently pleaded for attention and relief. But no-one offered such relief. Fun became torture.

It was not long before Jed's face was expressing the agony that, on a previous occasion, it had taken him hours to reveal.

One particularly cruel boy held his face an inch away from Jed's cock, and breathed warmly over it. Jed struggled to manoeuvre himself into the boy's mouth, but the ropes binding him to the cage only tightened. He simply could not move. The boy was so beautiful, his lips so warm and thick, his face so finely drawn... And forever out of reach.

'Please!' Jed groaned. 'Please help me!'

Before him, a growing group of boys was fucking, sucking and jerking off. An orgy on the grass. Every cock was getting some relief. Except his.

Wendell continued shooting long after he had got his required footage. Hell, he was enjoying this scene too much to allow it to stop. And he saw that he was not alone.

A glance at Russ Schlagrfarn, however, revealed that there was still more work to be done in that direction. Whilst around him every man was either masturbating, sucking, groping or fucking, Russ Schlagfarn, the richest man in Texas, was fast asleep, his false teeth gradually slipping from his mouth.

'CUT!' yelled Wendell.

Eager hands slipped Jed from his bonds. His immediate act was to rush into the arms of the first available boy who quickly took hold of his cock and jerked him off into quick, gasping relief.

Judy Garbo approached Wendell to offer congratulations:

Paradise Palace

'That was great! But I thought someone told me that this was to be The Tempest by William Shakespeare? I'm something of a Shakespeare fan, and I don't quite recall this scene in the oeuvre.'

'To hell with the erv!' snarled Wendell. 'This is Shakespeare Restored. Wipe away the dust and misinterpretations of centuries and this is what you're left with. We've had the original texts flown out from Oxford, England, so there's no-one can tell us we're wrong. This is Shakespeare as he intended. For the Common Man.'

'This is fascinating! I...'

But before Judy could launch into intellectual discourse, Wendell strode away. He wasn't going to indulge in any goddamn debate with some jumped-up North Eastern lawman.

Later. A deserted cloisters surrounding a quadrangle in the West Wing of the Palace. Wendell and Jed talk beside a marble pillar.

Wendell: Do not forget what I have charged thee with.
Jed: I'll do it, boss. Just give me time, hey?
Wendell: The boy must die.
Jed: I'll do it, alright? Don't bug me. It's you who's taken up all my time with this filming business.
Wendell: Remember Chicago.
Jed: Toby will be dead before the week is out, I swear.
Wendell: You have the poison. Do the deed.
Jed: It's as good as done.
Wendell: You're going far, boy. Real far.
Jed: Thanks, boss. Just give me time.

They parted: Wendell to his room, Jed to the fountain in the centre of the quadrangle. He sat on the edge and trailed his fingers in the water. Then he produced a small phial from the pocket of his jeans. He held it up to the light. A little grey powder. Nothing more. He unscrewed the cap. Tip it all into the water, Jed. Get rid of it, he told himself.

No. He had too much to lose. The boy Toby would have to die. Hell, what better to go than when you were young and happy? Why wait for old age, jealousy, misery and arthritis? Go before the world turns sour. Jed himself had a theory that the human male was meant to mate and then instantly die in a state of supreme satisfaction - hence all this post-coital depression around that was causing the population of the US to consume Prozac by the sack load. The Black Widow spider ate her husband after he had fucked her good. And well happy he probably was about it. And it was the same with the Praying Mantis. The males mated and then were eaten.

'Yeah, Toby,' Jed murmured, clutching the phial in his fist, 'You are one lucky dude. I envy you. If things weren't looking so bright for me in the future I might even reserve a little of the contents of this here phial for myself.'

Jed sat in this position for a long time, enjoying the silence broken only by the plashing of the water and the sound of distant laughter. He became filled with a good sadness and felt wise, as only one who holds the ultimate fate of another can do.

'Hey, Toby,' he whispered. 'I'm only doing this because I love you. Yeah? You understand? I love you, Toby.'

Chapter Sixteen

'I'm sorry, sir,' said Washington, 'but Mr Greatorix has given strict instructions that he is not to be disturbed on any account.'

'Oh, for Chrissake!' roared Wendell, 'cut out the Mr Greatorix stuff! I need Sam for this movie and I need him now. It's been two days since his little accident - he must have recovered by now. My god, it was only auto-asphyxiation, for Chrissake - we've all been there. Have you told him I've been trying to see him?'

They were in the reception room. Washington was leaning over the desk, looking down at Wendell.

'Of course I've told him, sir.'

'And you've given him my notes?'

'I've done everything you asked of me, sir.'

'What does the doctor say about him?'

'Just that he needs to rest and that he can't be disturbed.'

'Who takes his food up to him?'

'Either myself or Curt.'

'This!' Wendell produced a hundred dollar bill, 'says that you let me take up his supper tonight.'

'Money is silent at the Paradise Palace, sir. We're not allowed to take bribes. It's part of our contract. As you know, we're only too happy to do anything the guests ask of us so long as it does not go beyond our own personal limits.'

'Don't give me quotes, Washington. And money is nowhere silent. Sooner or later everyone starts to hear it.'

He began to place more hundred dollar bills on the counter. 'Two hundred, three, four, seven, eight...'

'Please, sir, this is not what we like to see at the Palace. Someone might come in and it would create a bad impression. All our guests are considerably wealthy and usually they don't like to see large amounts of money lying around. They think it lacks dignity.'

'A thousand dollars has more dignity than a dead Queen of

England!'

'Please.'

'This is your ticket out of here, boy.'

'I'm happy here, sir. I wouldn't stay if I wasn't. Sam looks after all of us very well. This is a happy place.'

'Oh, for Chrissake, don't give me that Winnie the Pooh stuff! Happy place! Two thousand dollars says I get to take Uncle Sam up his supper. If you like, I'll get my boy, Jed, to overpower you and tie you up so that steers you clear of any blame.'

'I'm sorry. But we function here on loyalty and trust. That's just how it is. Please put away that money, now. I'm afraid someone might come in.'

'You are one Little Miss Priss.'

'My name is Washington Bryars and I work for Sam Greatorix.'

'He must pay you boys pretty damn good. Eh? Eh?'

'This is a comfortable position,' Washington acknowledged.

'You bet your life.'

Abruptly, Wendell snatched up his money and began to walk away. When he was halfway to the door, he turned. 'Tell me something, boy. Is your boss - your Sam - in love, d'ya think? Has he been spending time with Toby?'

Washington inclined his head slightly. He was not sure how much Wendell knew about the situation regarding Toby, and he had to be careful not to let anything slip.

'Sam is unwell, sir,' he said. 'He doesn't leave his room. He cannot leave his room. Doctor's orders.'

'So does the boy, Toby, come to him?'

'No, sir.'

'But he's in love with that boy, ain't he?'

Washington's spontaneous answer surprised even himself: 'We're all in love with Sam, sir, and I dare say most of us like to think that that feeling might be reciprocated.'

'Whadda ya know?' wondered Wendell. And, appalling cynic that he was, he nevertheless felt something touch his heart. Hitherto, his

Paradise Palace

numerous notes to Sam had been rather perfunctory and almost aggressive - along the lines of "Come on, baby, I can give you all you want and more... My cock can reach where few others can ever hope to... Let's talk about the finer points of Shakespeare and shag each other senseless..." Things like that.

But now he went away and composed what was almost a tender letter. It contained a Shakespeare sonnet, a reflection on the 53rd psalm, a passing reference to a Bach motet (Wachet auf) and a drawing of an oasis of exquisite beauty in the Syrian desert, which Wendell owned.

"My dearest Sam," the letter began in an ornate hand that Wendell had learnt from his great grandmother. And it ended: "You know my feelings towards you, and if I may be sometimes clumsy in how I express them, put it down to the gaucheness of one whose emotions are too full to be confined by the narrow constraint of language. Marry me, Sam. We could honeymoon in the Syrian desert and read classical Arabic poetry by the light of the moon. I would not be possessive. You could have your little adventures with boys and I would sit at home knitting by the fireside. To be with you every day and to discuss philosophy and the meaning of life with someone who matches my intelligence - that's what I want as I come to this latter stage of my life. You must want it, too. I cannot believe that you don't. Boys satisfy an irritating itch - that's all. We need something deeper and more long-lasting. Isn't that so?

"This letter comes through Washington. His faithfulness as your servant deserves some recognition. You are surrounded by goodness. I hope you appreciate it.

"Sam, I send this letter with all my love and hope for a favourable reply.

"I am yours,

"Wendell T Banks."

Washington delivered the letter as requested. What he did not tell Wendell was that all his previous letters lay unopened on Sam's desk.

Sam sat all day on his throne and regarded the video screen. He moved only to go the bathroom and to his bed for snatches of sleep.

His life was devoted to watching. And, like most people who become obsessed, his thoughts strayed and occasionally fed on unpleasant parts of his psyche.

Would it be best to kill Toby? he wondered. The dead Toby would remain forever perfect, forever out of reach of the clammy hands of other men. Dead Toby would never grow old. His skin would never grow slack, muscles never become weak, mind never become cynical.

In his terrible isolation, this dreadful notion came to Sam to seem more and more reasonable. If Toby were dead, Sam would, in a way, possess him forever. And he, Sam, would be free once more to go about his daily business. Whilst he lived, Toby condemned Sam to this throne and this watch. It was not a happy state of affairs. And neither was Toby happy. Of course, he wasn't. Imprisoned and away from the company of his friends and lovers. And what greater joy could youth ultimately want than death? To die at the point of your greatest triumph as a human being! To die happy! That was surely what every man wanted.

If longing was what Sam truly wanted, then, what could be more perfect than to long for someone who was dead? Eternal longing: there was such perfection in that notion. People would say (as he passed them like a shadow outside the café window or on the deck of a cruise liner), 'There goes Sam Greatorix. The only boy he ever loved died at the age of eighteen, and since then his heart has been stone.'

Sam began to chew the length of his right forefinger - a habit that, if he were sitting next to you on a bus or subway train, would drive you to fury.

Murder does present problems. Like fucking underwater, it is nice in theory but tricky in practise. Of course, Sam would not be able to carry out the deed himself. Nor could he ask any of his boys. They were all so loyal and good and eager to please, none would refuse; but it would not be fair to ask. For one thing, no boy would necessarily like to become an assassin - the term 'murderer' still held a certain stigma for some people, after all - and for another, Sam was not sure that any of

Paradise Palace

his boys would understand the glorious concept of death. The young these days all thought of death as something horrid and to be avoided at all costs. Its romantic aspects were no longer given consideration. Ah, to be back in the time of the ancient Greeks where an early death - preferably on the battlefield in the arms of the soldier who was your best love - was what all young men most earnestly longed for! Boys loved life, these days, which was not necessarily a pity, but it did mean that this loved life lacked a certain romantic edge.

If he could not do the thing himself - oh, no, perish the thought! - and could not call upon any of his faithful servants, whom could he ask? He did not want to hire a hit-man (although there was a gay agency that he had once used years back, for very different reasons, based in Houston, that generally provided a very reliable service) because that would be too cold and clinical.

How about Wendell Banks? No, that wouldn't be right. He hardly knew the guy, and he couldn't rely on him to keep his mouth shut. Doctor Max? No. He wouldn't do it. The Hippocratic Oath forbade doctors from taking the life of another. Then who?

When finally he alighted on the name of one who might oblige, it seemed obvious. Of course. He should have thought of him in the first place.

Sam leant over the arm of his throne and pressed a button on the intercom:

'Washington? Washington, I want you to find that Jed Howitzer and send him up to me. It's urgent. Tell him I want him right away.'

'Sure thing, chief!'

Sam turned back to the video screen. Using the hand-held tuner he adjusted the focus of the camera and examined the sleeping boy in close detail: the ring of tiny spots around each nipple, the mole beside his navel, every fold and crevice of his genitals. The eye of the camera caressed the boy and presented an image of perfection. This, without sound or scent or awkwardness, was what would remain: the true essence of boy.

The bell - or, rather, bells, being a peal based on the song 'Mad About

The Boy' - rang. Sam saw who it was on the entry screen and called, 'Enter!'

'I'm an old man, Jed, and I won't beat about the bush because time - every beat, every moment, every second - is precious at my age. I have a favour to ask of you.'

Jed grinned and his hand ran down the bulge in his jeans. With his pecs and biceps straining out of a too-tight tee-shirt and his cock outlined like a cosh beneath his trousers, he looked more like an animated Tom of Finland poster than a real human being.

'Name it, Sam!' Having been called 'way too old' and 'past it' by Sam on his arrival, Jed was now delighted to have the guy call upon him for, as he thought, sexual favours. 'I can do anything. I was voted "Best Head-Giver in Dixie" only last year, at the annual convention of Gay Relief Workers in New Orleans. And if I let you in on the secret, that my nickname is "Motor Tongue", that might give you some idea of my particular prowess. A lot of training went into that, and I'm proud of it. And that's not all, of course. My cock has been measured by top experts and only a couple of years ago, I was crowned - or rather, it was crowned Top Cock in Alabama 1995... It's also won awards for length and endurance in Tennessee, Mississippi, Louisiana and Des Moines. I'm also a big hit out West, as you probably know, and at the biennial ball-weighing contest in...'

'Oh, for Chrissake, shut-up! There's no way that I'm gonna let your ageing body go down on me. You didn't turn me on when you first arrived and you never will. All that great dong stuff disgusts me completely and to see you in those goddamn jeans almost makes me want to vomit. I like what's natural and your pumped-up body oozes falsity and corruption.'

The voice from the throne had spoken and Jed felt as if he had just received an icy blast. If Sam had been looking, he would have noticed a considerable automatic shrinking of Jed's fabulous cock as the thing crept back for safety's sake.

'I didn't call you here because I wanted your sexual services - whatever gave you that idea?'

Paradise Palace

Then, seeing Jed's crestfallen expression, Sam's tone softened. He did not want to offend the boy - that would not be good politics.

'Aw, gee, kid, I'm sorry. You've caught me at a touchy time in my life, is all. I'm an old man, and things don't get any easier when you get to my age. You're young and beautiful, it's hard for you to imagine that such an age as sixty-eight exists, but it does, and here it is, sitting before you.'

'You're looking beautiful on it, sir. And, if I may say so, I could desire you, if only you would allow me.'

It was true - Sam was an exceptionally handsome man, and Jed found such men enormously attractive.

Sam waved a dismissive hand. 'Sweet of you to say so; but, well, the desires of the flesh have less appeal for me now than once they did. Jed, I want to ask you a direct question. What's the most that anyone's ever offered you to perform a favour - any sort of favour? Come on. Answer me straight. I won't bite your head off.'

Jed hesitated a moment. Then, 'Ten thousand dollars,' he answered truthfully.

Sam's expression did not change, 'Was that easy money?'

'No, sir.'

'You know, I teach my boys here - and we're like a family with myself at the head - that it is beneath our dignity to talk about money. I hate the expression "Money talks". Hate it. It's vulgar. None of my boys is allowed to accept bribes. They're well looked after. We had a client once, heh, heh, heh,' he chuckled, 'who couldn't perform unless he paid the boy personally each time. And ya know what? He only went with this one boy the whole duration of his stay, and each time he paid this boy, that boy then came to me and handed over the money - voluntarily, he didn't have to, none of us would have known of that particular quirk, otherwise. The boy could have kept silent and kept all the money. Instead, he handed it over. And you can be sure that when that guest went back home, I gave the boy all those bonus earnings - and some - as a reward. Money is vulgar, but, I grant, it can be useful. Jed, I want you to perform a small favour for me, and if you'll do it I'll guarantee you twenty thousand dollars. It might, or might not, be easy money. Everything is subjective.'

There followed a long silence, during which Sam stared at a video screen. Jed followed the direction of Sam's eyes. But nothing was revealed: the screen was blank.

'What did you have to do for your ten thousand?'

'I'm sorry, sir. I can't reveal that.'

'Nobly said. I respect you for that. I'll come straight to the point, Jed. I'm a big man in this world. A major shareholder in SunBoys International - the publishing company that I believe brings out all the titles in which you've appeared. I've also got interests in BlueWorld - the company who put up most of the funding for the films you make with Wendell Banks. What do you think all that means?'

'That you're rich?'

'And then some. And money is pleasant in itself, but it also brings with it some small advantages on the side. Power for one. If you have a little money, people can't shit on you. It gives you that freedom. It's worth having. Twenty thousand dollars would give you at least a taste of that, Jed. Power. Because my money gives me power over you, right now. If I so wanted, I could finish your career in five minutes. A couple of phone calls. That's all it would take. "Jed Howitzer has offended me. If he appears once more in any of your films or publications I'm going to sell my shares to the Vatican."'

The conversation was taking an unpleasant turn. Jed swallowed nervously.

'What would you have me do, sir?' he asked, using the stock phrase and frail voice that he adopted when confronted with a client who wanted to practise a little sadism.

In answer, Sam produced a small glass phial from a pocket of his robe. He held it up to the light. It contained a grey powder.

'Do you know what this is?'

As a matter of fact, Jed certainly did know. But he could hardly admit to the fact.

'It's a little substance manufactured from one of our friends in the

Paradise Palace

toadstool family. Amanita Foscurum. Let me tell you what it can do...'
Jed made an effort to conceal a wry smile.

Peter Slater

Chapter Seventeen

That night, Jed dreamt. He dreamt dollar bills - money falling languidly from the sky. There he was, striding along, gathering it up and bundling it into sacks. 'Easy money!' he said to himself. Easy-peasy, lemon-squeezy!

He sailed, in a small boat made out of greenbacks, to a paradise island populated by a thousand gay boys. They swam out to him, and the churning sea was full of laughing faces and lithe bodies. Soon, they were trying to clamber into the boat - cocks erect, water streaming from smooth skin and slicked back hair. But the boat proved frail and each time a boy grabbed one of the sides, that side bent and let in the water. Pretty soon, Jed was battling to keep afloat. The boys thought all this was great fun - but not Jed, who could not swim. Of course you can swim! they responded to his panicked cries. Everyone can swim! Come on in, get a piece of the action! No matter how much Jed protested, no-one took any notice. Water began to fill the hold and Jed started to bail out with a tiny paper beaker made out of yet another dollar bill. It was useless.

A red and green parrot landed on the mast. It held out one wing and spoke, 'Money can't save your skin! Money can't save your skin!'

'Get lost, little buddy!' Jed roared.

The parrot shrugged its wings as much as to say, He who does not listen to parrots is lost, and flew away. At the last minute, knowing that if he could only touch the bird he would be able to fly to safety, Jed reached out and made a grab for its claws. But he was too late and missed. The violent action caused him to lose balance and he fell into the water. Eager hands reached for him; and, briefly, as he felt firm fingers on his cock and balls, Jed thought himself saved. The feeling was not to last. He was like a stone statue in the water. And the water rose up around him, smothering his face like a layer of film. No matter how much he struggled, he could not keep his head above water. Images of sweet life tumbled through his mind: sunlight flowing through the branches of a tree, a ride in an open-top car along the California coast-line, downing a can of cold beer after a day's hard work, making love with a lion-tamer in a cage of wild beasts... He writhed and gasped and called out...

'Yarscchh!' cried Jed, surfacing into wakefulness.

He was soaking. For a moment he mistook his sweat for sea-water, until he re-established his bearings. A good, dry bed. He stared up at the ceiling and took deep breaths. Aw, gosh, it was good to be alive! Dear, sweet life. And, for the first time, he began to have real doubts as to what he had been asked to do. Up until now, he had viewed the whole enterprise in rather technical terms: murder was awful, but somehow he had not fully appreciated how terrible a thing it was - you read about it every day in the papers, and saw it in the movies. Sure, it could give you a jolt from time to time, but he had always rated it on a par with having a bad fuck or being busted for drugs: pretty awful, but hardly the end of the world. Murder, loss of life, had lacked reality. It was an abstract notion, as death itself was an abstract notion. Now, though, so real had been that dream, he was forced to confront the fact that death was appalling and painful. 'I can't do it!' he thought.

And yet, he knew that if he did not do it, his life, his career would be over. Sam would get him from one angle, Wendell from another. And he wasn't one of Mother Nature's brightest stars. Once he went into freefall, he would not be able to save himself through the strength of his wits. He would go down and down and end up in the gutter. Performing tricks for nervous businessmen down by the pier. Ten dollars a time, if he was lucky. A knife in the guts, if he wasn't.

The telephone by his bed began to trill.

'Jed Howitzer speaking.'

'Russ Schlagfarn,' came a breathy voice. 'I am consumed by desire.'

The phrase may have been a little quaint, but there was nothing quaint about the dollar signs that now appeared in glorious Technicolor before Jed's eyes. His heart beat faster, and he sat up.

Peter Slater

'Oh, Russ, honey, baby, I'm just longing for you...'

'Yeah, well, cut out the crap and get over here fast - and bring some elastic bands, I'll need a tourniquet, sure as hell.'

'I'll be right there, sir! Think of a fantasy! Think of me covered in chocolate!'

Jed shot out of bed and into a pair of briefs. Then hunted in his suitcase for elastic bands. It wasn't an unheard of request and he kept a good supply of a multicoloured variety. He grabbed a couple of cock-rings and a leather strap, as well.

Within five minutes, Jed, wearing only his white briefs and a thin gold chain round his neck, was standing outside Russ Schlagfarn's door. He paused to get his breath back and rearrange his genitals more comfortably. A little massage to give a slight, welcoming erection. He knocked: peremptory yet discreet (the watchwords of any hooker).

'Enter!'

The sight that met his eyes was horrific: as if he had come upon a demented transvestite surgeon midway through his life's mission of trying to wreak revenge on the world's genitals.

Russ Schlagfarn was lying naked on his double bed whilst Judy Garbo hovered over his blood-spattered penis with a carving knife.

'Judy, what the hell!' Jed rushed forward.

'Nyarrr! Have a carrot, doc!' urged Bugs from the perpetual cartoon on the wall.

'We're too late,' said Judy. 'It's all over.

'What happened? What's happening?'

It transpired that, lacking elastic bands, Russ Schlagfarn had tied string around the base of his penis in order to maintain the precious erection. Judy - who had been summoned as an essential witness to the hoped-for grand event - had arrived in time to see Russ struggling to untie clumsy knots whilst his cock turned a deep shade of blue. The only thing to hand had been a carving knife and Judy had no alternative but to begin cutting. Unfortunately, what with Russ's struggling and his own nervousness, his aim had not been that good.

'It's all over!' Russ repeated Judy's melancholy words. 'And it was a beauty, too! Solid as a tree trunk! Ya know, the ironic thing was that I think it would have stayed in position of its own accord; but I panicked and went for the string. Big mistake. Big mistake. One thing's for sure - I won't even be able to contemplate any action for a few days until the scars heal. Ah, well! The cookie crumbles, and all that.'

'Nyarrr! Bad luck, doc!' consoled Bugs.

Wendell Banks was sitting on his canvas director's chair in the shade of a large Casuarina tree outside the walls of the palace. He was reading Civil War News. Beside him, on blankets, were his sound recordist and cameraman. They were playing 'My Old Kentucky Home' on banjo and penny whistle.

'Hi, boss! We shooting today?' Jed asked, as he approached.

Wendell looked up. There were tears in his eyes.

'The old times,' he said. 'What happened?'

'They freed the slaves, boss.' Jed was used to his master's maudlin moments.

'Them slaves had dignity, boy.'

'I don't deny that, boss; but…'

'And they had dignity because they were slaves. Once Lincoln let 'em go, anarchy and chaos reigned. My great-great grandfather was a slave and I can always remember my grandfather telling me how his pappy was so sorry to have to leave his owner on the old plantation.'

Wendell always preferred romance to fact; and, for him, all history (provided it was safely tucked up a hundred years in the past) was romantic. He was not insensitive, he could understand the suffering of the here and now; but for him, life on "the old plantation" - all moonlight and low spirituals - only evoked warm feelings.

His weirdest film - and perhaps the weirdest movie in history - was called A Thousand Slave Boys and featured just those, in a vast Louisiana mansion in the heart of a swamp. They loyally served a cruel white master, his brothers, sons and wives; until, when the Civil War came, they went into battle against the yankee soldiers and succeeded in seducing an entire battalion. The final scenes featured Lincoln himself succumbing to the charms of a negro hunk called Matatooli. Not only was the great president featured in various sexual situations, but he was shown being taken around a bizarrely happy plantation full of singing slaves, chopping cane, and was heard to declare, 'I say now, before all America, I was wrong!'

Another of Wendell's movies, Runaway Slaves, starred a slave boy shackled to his young white master (for reasons never made entirely clear in the narrative). Their adventures in the woods and barns of Alabama helped make this one of the top-grossing gay movies of 1992.

Jed sat down next to the musicians and patiently waited for his boss to recover his senses. Eventually, the music stopped and Wendell, nodding slowly as if paying obeisance to a greater, invisible force, said that yes, there would be filming today. Had Jed mugged up on the script?

'Sure!' Jed lied.

'It doesn't matter, anyway.' Wendell saw through him. 'You don't have any lines, beyond a few natural groans here and there. It's all a continuation of your labours to win Prospero's slave-boy's cock. We'll have to drive up to the mountains, though, to get the right atmosphere. Feeling up to it?'

'With you, boss - any time!'

'You're a sweetie!'

Wendell, holding a long staff that towered above him, and wearing a matching robe and floppy hat patterned with stars, moons, suns and signs of the zodiac, stood on top of a boulder and pointed to Jed below.

'Thou hast done well thus far, vagrant slave! But henceforth, thy tasks grow ever harder. Your next trial is to seek out the wild boys who inhabit the farthest corners of this island. When thou hast found them, thou must gather their magic cum in a vessel I shall give thee. Then, thou must bring it back to me. It has great powers for good and ill, and I need it for my experiments. But, be warned! The boys do not surrender themselves easily to the advances of strangers, and if they take a dislike to thee they will rape and kill thee. Also, thou should'st know that after mating with a stranger they oft do kill him merely for sport. What sayst thou? Art up to the challenge?'

'Sure thing, boss!'

'CUT! You'll be the death of me, Jed, ya really will! Don't say anything, just nod. Hey?'

Later that night, a small crowd gathered in the room set aside as Wendell's temporary studio, to watch the rough cuts of the movie thus far. That day's filming certainly featured some of the best moments hitherto.

Jed, alias Ferdinand, his face and torso streaked with a mystical swirling pattern of red and blue, peered from behind a bush. His eyes were intent on something - or someone - which was yet hidden from the viewer. He was excited - the camera focused on his right hand as it nuzzled his loin cloth. What had he seen?

The next shot revealed two young savages bathing in a rock pool. One was intent on examining the other's scalp for fleas. This was an action featured in all of Wendell's movies - one of his own greatest joys was to have his scalp picked over by sensitive fingers, and he was right to imagine that the more sophisticated members of his public enjoyed watching such scenes. Back home, in Oxford, Mississippi, he visited his scalp picker (not masseur, he always went to great pains to stress) at least once a week.

Despite the slowness of their movements and the apparent lack of any major sexual arousal, the film conveyed something of their unrestrained animal power. Wendell was a great director, and he had also cast the parts well. These two boys were played by Swing and Swung, the native Americans, and they took to their roles naturally.

Ferdinand was clearly becoming very excited by the careful sensuality of these wild boys. With a casual twist of his fingers he freed his cock and began to masturbate using thumb and two fingers.
And now the boys were also showing some signs of arousal. Swing, who was doing the picking, allowed his fingers to stray over his

brother's face. Swung opened his mouth and caught Swing's right forefinger with his tongue. The camera closed in on the finger being licked and caressed by the tongue and nibbled by perfect white teeth. And when the finger started to fuck the mouth, squeezing in through thick, moist lips, the effect was as sensual as witnessing an actual fucking with genitals.

The next shot showed them twined in a deep, passionate kiss. A close up of their faces. A close up of their cocks pressed together and being masturbated by one hand. Then Ferdinand, by now heavily involved in self-stimulation, lost his balance. There was a loud cracking of twigs. The boys looked up startled.

The next scenes were of the boys, cocks erect and daggers at the ready, searching the undergrowth for intruders. When they found Ferdinand, their first actions were to threaten violence, and a fight ensued. Pretty soon, however, when they had established their superior strength and held Ferdinand in a painful arm-lock, he used his free hand to massage Swing's cock and it was apparent from the expression of ecstasy on his face that matters were going to progress peacefully. Swung let go of Ferdinand, and he fell forward on his knees and began licking the area between Swing's arse and the base of his penis. Swung rose and, whilst snogging his brother, began to masturbate him.

The orgy that followed ended with Ferdinand slipping condoms over the two boys' cocks and then, doggy-fashion, offering his arse for a balletic double fuck. The film avoided most of the awkward manoeuvring, but closed in as the cocks, one atop the other, began the penetration.

Ferdinand's expression of joyful agony was not an act, and neither were the screams and cries of the boys as they plunged faster and faster into the tightest fuck of their young lives. They came almost simultaneously, their bodies quivering with emotion.

The final scene showed the boys sleeping and Ferdinand picking up their filled condoms and disappearing off into the forest. His task complete.

Chapter Eighteen

Sam sat in his robes, immobile on his throne, chin propped on his right hand. The Emperor paralysed whilst his Empire began to go adrift. The movement was thus far almost imperceptible; but, if action were not taken, there might soon be consequences. There were things he needed to do, urgent matters that required his attention. Papers needed to be signed, letters needed to be written, people had to be spoken to. The local Sheriff was expecting a donation towards his campaign fund for re-election; donations should never be forgotten, memory-lapses tended to lead to eventualities that could be unpleasant. A certain senator needed a friendly phone-call to remind him that there were certain photographs on file, so it might be as well if he were to back-pedal on the current 'Clean Up Arizona' drive.

Forget the notion that the world consists of maybe one or two superpowers and perhaps a few dozen smaller countries. In fact, there are myriad empires and kingdoms. Institutions, businesses, families: they are all independent states needing government and strong leadership. And when that government weakens or is absent, then the very existence of the state may be threatened. Some of these states, of course, may be relatively democratic, with the power spread amongst a number of people: the chances of these collapsing is, perforce, not so great. But for those oligarchies or dictatorships, where power is held by only a few, the outlook, in the event of unforeseen catastrophe afflicting the leadership, is not so good.

Sam Greatorix was the only power at the Paradise Palace. He was President, King, Emperor, Tsar. There was no devolution of power whatsoever. He never took a holiday, never fell ill, was never absent from his post. He had helpers and aides, of course; and he listened to good advice. But all decisions, all the oilings and workings, wheelings and dealings of state came from him, and him alone.

So his absence made a difference. Small things began to go wrong. A guest, dissatisfied with a less than perfect crème caramel at dinner and flying into a rage, was not mollified by the apologies of the chef; he demanded to see the manager. There was no manager available. The guest left the following day, vowing never to return. Such a small pocket of ill-will should never have been allowed to form. Sam would have put the guest to rights with not only the right sort of apology, but also through application of wise psychology. No man could really get upset over a crème caramel; the true problem must lie elsewhere. The blameless dish clearly stood as the tangible expression of some form of sexual inability. The man had not been fuming either at his sweet or at the chef, but rather at his limp penis, which had failed him the night before. Sam would have detected this and sent him along a boy trained in sex therapy. A couple of orgasms later, and uniform joy would have been restored throughout the palace. It didn't happen. A pool of darkness was created and, as is the way with these things, spread a little; so that, however faintly, the sense that all was not quite right began to seep through the entire palace.

The Emperor sat and watched his boy. Who slept and woke, ate and paced the room like a caged animal.

Sam summoned Jed.

'When will you do what I have asked?'

'Soon, sir. It's difficult, ya know.'

'I don't know. Your problems are not mine. When will you do what I have asked?'

'Soon, sir.'

'Soon is not a time. Name a time.'

'I…'

'Name a time.'

'Tomorrow evening.'

Sam Greatorix pulled his head back and took a deep breath through his nostrils. 'Thank you,' he said. 'Tomorrow evening. You may go.'

Jed hesitated a moment, then turned abruptly and exited the room. He had another appointment to keep.

Wendell was hanging naked from the harness in the ceiling of his room.

Paradise Palace

'Sam is still in his room,' he told Jed, who was sitting in a white armchair luxuriously stuffed with down. 'The word is that the boy, Toby, is still alive. Why is he still alive, Jed?'

'I haven't had time to do anything yet, boss.'

'You don't need "time" to sprinkle a little powder. It's the work of five minutes to pop down to the kitchens, find which plate is his and do the deed.'

'But I've gotta be careful not to raise any suspicions, boss.'

'Amanita Foscurum allows no room for suspicion. It leaves all the symptoms of a heart attack. Teenage boys are passing out all over the world with the same thing - how many times do I have to tell ya?'

'But...'

'No "buts"! When're ya gonna do it?'

'Tomorrow night.'

'I've got your word on that?'

'You got my word.'

'You're a good boy, Jed. You'll go far. Now help me down outa this thing, will ya? - my toes are losing blood.'

Despite the heavy weight upon his shoulders, Jed performed brilliantly during the next day's filming, and they got through many pages of script. Wendell had come up with the idea that Jed's lines be spoken as voice-over and be dubbed on later, so all the boy had to do was act - or, rather, make love in the manner dictated by the labours accorded him by Prospero. The day passed pleasantly, with plenty of coital groans and lashings of cum. Shakespeare, himself, would have been proud.

Like an overexcited virgin, night comes quickly in the desert. One moment there is full sunlight, then in the next, as at the turning of a switch, there is darkness.

A huge, white pockmarked moon hung so low in a black sky you might have thought it possible to reach out and clamber onto it. It threw benevolent silver light onto canyon and butte, cactus and mese.

There was a legend in this part of the desert of a ghost boy who haunted the caves and canyons. The gay son of an Apache chief, he had been murdered by his jealous brothers, and his spirit, instead of drifting off to the happy hunting grounds, had decided to stay around on earth - because it was more fun than chasing elk in the other world full of goody-goody happy spirits. Wolf-boy, as he was known, wanted mischief and wild sex, and you don't get that in Apache Heaven, where death is lived according to a very politically-correct handbook.

The weekly night-time wolf-boy trips were a part of the essential itinerary for the more adventurous among the Paradise Palace clientele. Small groups were led out into the desert at the stroke of midnight and treated to camp fire ghost stories, told by some of the more theatrically-minded boys. With cold beer or wine and barbecued chicken and steak, this was a treat in itself. But further delights awaited those even braver souls who chose to venture away from the firelight and into the shadow-filled hinterland of boulder and rock. Back there lay the possibility that a slither of thicker shadow might prove to be more tangible. The slight touch of a hand, a faint warm breath, a whisper. What was that? A man might put out his hand and trace the smooth skin of an Indian ghost boy: the chest, thighs, low-hung balls and long pulsing cock. Ghost or not, those men who returned with the cum of a teenage Apache boy on their faces, were always more than happy with the experience.

Now, it so happened that this night that Jed had chosen to carry out the murder coincided with one of the wolf-boy expeditions. Ordinarily, this would have made no difference; but this particular excursion was heavily oversubscribed and, in order that as many as possible might enjoy a chance encounter with the other world, several extra boys were needed as volunteers to play the part of the sexually-voracious ghost. The kitchen, especially, found itself short-staffed - a disproportionate number of its staff were of Indian blood.

The chef, a highly strung, hugely overweight Neapolitan, in white uniform and hat, toddled through the corridors of the palace, lamenting

Paradise Palace

loudly and demanding to see Sam Greatorix.

He came upon Curt at the reception desk:

'Get me Mr Sam! I cannota cook a decent supper withouta my helpers and now they all disappear to play ghosts!'

Curt nervously patted the air with the palms of his hands, 'Cool it, Giuseppi! Cool it! We don't want the guys around here to know that the ghost boy ain't real!'

'What's itta matter to them whether the kid is real or not? They know he's notta real!'

'Sure, they know it. But they still like to pretend, and we mustn't do anything to puncture that pretence. Too much reality's bad for a man.'

'I needa help! Not all our guests have gone out on this wilda goose chase.'

By good fortune, just at that moment, Jed came up.

'I could lend you a hand in the kitchen,' he offered.

And, as he spoke, a cold flower bloomed inside his stomach.

Chapter Nineteen

A desolate soul hovers like a grey mist above a solitude of ice and snow.

'I'll take that one, Giuseppi!' said Jed

In the steamy kitchen in the basement of the palace, Giuseppi was arranging a plate of seafood for the prisoner in the dungeon - 'The Count of Monte Christo', he called him.

'No, no! It'sa all right! One of the boy's guards willa come to collect.'

'Oh, let me take it. It's fresh on the plate, it'll spoil if you have to leave it hanging about.'

'No, thank you. I need you here. Look - stirra that sauce in that pan, will you? Quick! It'sa getting lumpy.'

Jed obeyed, but kept glancing from plate to door. At any minute, Toby's guard might come through and pick up the plate and his chance would be gone.

'I'll take it,' he repeated. 'I mean, after all, the poor kid's locked away down there - he deserves fresh food.'

'The fooda will be fresh. A coupla minutes give or take will makea no difference.'

'Don't give me that! You know the difference a small amount of time makes to the quality of a fresh seafood salad.'

Giuseppi looked up and his eyes (the colour of succulent Tuscan blackcurrants) met Jed's (the colour of succulent Idaho blueberries). International Berrytime at the Paradise Palace. Otherwise known as the season of epiphany.

'You'rea in love!' he exclaimed. 'The grreata Jed Howitzer is in lerrv!' The final verb took on a weird French intonation, as if only such a pronunciation could do justice to its dramatic quality.

Jed blushed, and it was as if the true nature of his pleading had indeed been revealed.

'Hah!' The Italian clapped his hands together with a loud crack!

Paradise Palace

'Now I know it! Everyone issa falling in lerrv witha this boy. Sssss! It'sa pathetic!' He turned back to his arrangement of lettuce and endive. 'The palace issa full of boys and you all go mooning after one!'

'Can't be helped,' Jed said softly, seeing his opening.

Giusseppi raised his head again, 'Letta me give you some advicea! Don'ta touch the boy. Sammy, he wantsa heem forra his own. He'lla keel any rivals…'

'I just need to be near him, Giusseppi. I want to breathe the same air that's been inside him. I want the same air that's caressed his naked body to caress mine.'

'Madre Mio! You havea caught it bad!'

'Please, Giusseppi!' Jed took out his cock and flopped it on the table beside the cook. 'All this is yours,' he said, like a king giving his crown prince a new domain. 'Whenever and however.'

Giusseppi hid a natural shudder at the sight of this lump of uncooked sausage meat. Giusseppi was a man with a secret. He was a happily married man with a wife and five kids back in Naples. He had never felt the slightest attraction towards any man or boy, but he kept this hidden because Sam paid extraordinarily well. Heterosexuality was way too bizarre a practise for the Paradise Palace, and any employee found harbouring this odd inclination would find himself out of a job pretty quick. So Giusseppi affected a staunch celibacy. He was, he proclaimed, an N.P.H. - a non-practising-homosexual. When asked why, he always said, 'Blamea the Pope!' And his interlocutors always went away, shaking their heads and muttering about the appalling repression that the Roman Catholic church exerted, even in this day and age and place. One day soon, he would return to Italy and take early retirement in considerable comfort. But in the meantime, here was this cock. Giusseppi gave it a little pat, as you would a dachshund.

'It'sa verry beautiful' he congratulated. 'But not necessary fora me. I'm ana Italiano! - of course I understanda Romance and secret love! I havea been on the canals of Venezia and havea prowled like a tom cat through the back alleys of Napoli. Takea the boy hees supper! But I pray to you, be discreet. Sam is not his olda self and maya take

Peter Slater

badly to rivalry.'

'Don't worry, Giusseppi. I'll take good care.'

'There'sa cameras everywhere, don'ta forget! Sam, he'lla see your effery move.'

'Just a few moments in Toby's presence. That's all I want.'

Shaking his head at the folly of love, Giusseppi handed Jed the plate on a tray, wished him well and urged him to return swiftly - there was a lot of work that needed doing in the kitchens.

'Cheers, Giusseppi! You're a pal! And if ya should want my cock anytime…'

'Ciao, baby!'

Killing people is never, in the end, going to be a philosophy or practise promulgated by gays. Heck, we've seen too much of death. So many of our brightest and best have faded and dimmed and passed on before their time. To be gay is to cherish life. We love, not for the procreation of future generations, but merely for the sake of love itself: there is a sacred nobility in that.

Jed sat down on a bench in one of the corridors en route to Toby's cell and took out the phial of poison. He turned it over and over in his hands. And he remembered. He remembered Sandy and Andrew, Michael, Phillip, Paul, Bob, Jimmy, Jason… Hospital corridors, bunches of flowers. Jason, sitting up in bed - it was one of his good days. 'I've brought you something!' said Jed, suddenly giggly with relief. He held up a brown paper bag and put on his whimsical Stan Laurel face, 'Hard boiled eggs and nuts!' Distant voices and far-off laughter.

'Heya, Jason!' said Jed, lightly punching the air in the way that he had used to greet his old buddy.

He drew back his fist and uncurled it. It contained the glass phial.

Jed paused awhile - not thinking, but knowing. He stood up, went to a nearby bathroom and flushed both phials of Amanita Foscurum down the pan.

'Bang goes my fortune!' he murmured. 'But… But, yo! I'm happy!… In a sad way.'

Paradise Palace

Names, too, were going through Sam's mind: Jan, Peter, William, Rob, Harry, Gus, Bill, John, Trevor, Arthur, Simon, Fred, Steve... He couldn't remember them all. Sometimes he felt as if he were alone in a theatre after the show had finished and everyone had gone home. The music, the laughter, the applause were all gone. He turned around on his throne and regarded a framed photograph on one of his shelves. Bobbie's Gang, they had called themselves: just a regular bunch of guys who used to hang out in Bobbie's Bar on Norfolk Street, San Francisco. Charlie, Norman, Andrew, Malcolm, Richard, Liam, Paul, Michael... He had loved Michael. He had been a trumpet with the Los Angeles Philharmonic and had had a great story about once having sex in a broom cupboard with Leonard Bernstein: 'And this was barely ten minutes after we had finished Mahler's Ninth in the Philharmonic Hall!' Who was left from that crew? Only himself.

At first, he had crossed the names out in his address book. But then he could no longer bear to do that.

Sam stared at the floor.

Wendell Banks was sitting in his room working on his tapestry of The Battle of Gettysburg. He was an adept stitcher and particularly skilful at faces. The ugliness of the brutes who made up the Yankee army contrasted sharply with the beauty of the Confederates. He literally snarled when he had to depict a Yankee, but his face was wreathed with a benevolent smile when he came to a Fed.

'Mine eyes have seen the glory of the coming of the Lord!' he sang, oblivious to irony.

His mind was filled with easy fictional history - he hated to be troubled by uncomfortable facts. It was fun to believe in a lie, and the Civil War was a long time ago; no-one could be harmed now by whatever view you took of it.

But Wendell was not a fool. Sometimes it occurred to him that there was another Civil War raging right now. Sure, this one didn't have bombs or bullets, but it was just as deadly and just as horrible.

Peter Slater

This War set brother against brother, friend against friend, divided families. This War devastated communities and created silence where once was the sound of laughter. But this time the enemy was not other people: it was death itself.

You could joke about long-forgotten battles - time eventually erases all pain. But when the battles were taking place right now, it wasn't so easy.

'Real people,' Wendell murmured. 'My soldier boys ain't real. That Toby, though…' He lifted his eyes and gazed at the wall.

Jed was in the anteroom to Toby's cell and in the act of handing over the tray of food to Washington, Toby's jailer, when first Sam and then Wendell burst in with cries of 'No! Stop! Don't touch that plate!'

Jed was delighted at this show of humanity; it quite restored his faith.

Washington, though, was utterly confused, 'Hey, what is this?' he protested. 'Toby needs his supper!'

'Not this one he doesn't!' said Sam, picking up the plate and flinging it to the stone floor.

'Why'd you do that?' asked Washington.

'Salmonella in the kitchens.'

'Sure are!' agreed Wendell. 'They're swimmin' over everything!'

'Gee!' said Washington. 'Does that mean we're gonna haveta close the place down?'

'Yes!' said Sam, instantly. Then, 'No. I'll get Giuseppi to spray something. What're you doing here, Wendell?' He appeared to notice Wendell Banks for the first time.

'Uh, I heard the same thing. About the fish in the kitchen.'

'What?'

'Those deadly what-you-saids… All over. So I thought I'd better…'

There was a long pause. Washington began clearing up the mess.

'Wendell,' said Sam. 'Wendell. Come back to my room awhile,

will ya? I think we need ta do some talking.'

Both men disappeared.

Jed bent to help Washington.

'You any idea what all that was about?' asked Washington.

'I'm not sure,' Jed replied. 'But I think it might be something to do with love. These are interesting times.'

'Interesting times,' Washington echoed. 'You can sure say that one again!'

Chapter Twenty

Sitting side-by-side on Sam's emperor-sized bed, Wendell Banks and Sam Greatorix talked long into the night. Their conversation strayed over such topics as love and the meaning of love, sehnsucht (look it up in chapter thirteen if you've been rushing through and missing pages; there's more to life than the bits you're looking for, let this be a warning) and meaning, myth and magic in Wagner's Ring cycle.

Time led them into the most desolate parts of its being; but, the odd thing was, neither of them was afraid of 3 a.m. consciousness. Sam was discovering a companionship deeper than the temporary attraction of body; and Wendell - well, Wendell had it both ways: he adored Sam's mind and his body.

'Marry me, Sam!' Wendell dared offer at 3.45. 'It'll be the marriage of true minds. 'Marry me and be faithful and you'll get the best of all possible worlds: eternal longing (I'll never allow you to lay hands on Toby), great sex (I'm a fabulous lover), and communication with me on a deep emotional and intellectual basis. We'd also form a fabulous business partnership. We could film the whole of Shakespeare's gay canon! You and me together, forever and ever. It makes good sense.'

Sam looked across at the video screen on the wall. Toby was lying on his bed asleep. Sam reached for the remote-control, aimed it and fired. The picture vanished.

'Hell, I'm too old to marry! And, besides, I'm not the marrying type. Check out Zsa Zsa Gabor if ya wanna get hitched. Doris Day. Forget Sam Greatorix.'

'Ya know I can't do that, Sam. It's you I want, and you and me together would work. Hell, you're not too old! Octagenarians can marry! Nonagenarians! We're a perfect match. I knew it from the first…' Then Wendell's voice took on a more serious tone, 'Sam, I got a question.'

'Out with it.'

'Why'd ya throw Toby's plate on the floor?'

'I told ya - salmonella poisoning.'

Paradise Palace

'It wasn't because… because ya knew somethin' about me?'

'What d'ya mean?'

'I know ya got half the place fixed up on closed-circuit TV and I wondered if ya might have overheard a private conversation? Between me and Jed?'

'No, sir.'

An element of awkwardness had been introduced and an uncomfortable silence settled.

'What's this about?' asked Sam. 'Have you been talking to Jed?' Both now feared that Jed had told the other about the murder plot.

'Jed's a good friend of mine,' said Wendell.

'Are you blackmailing me?' asked Sam.

'No, sir.'

'Because I can't be had that way. If you want the truth, I'll tell ya the truth. I'm not gonna spend the rest of my life hiding a dark secret.'

'We've all got our dark secrets.' Wendell was becoming concerned about Sam's state of agitation. 'I don't wanna probe.'

'You're kinda sneaky, aren't ya?'

'No, sir. If you've got a past, that ain't no concern of mine. We've all got pasts. I could tell you something that would shock you and give you a hold over me - if you don't already know it. Which I'm beginning ta think you do.'

'I loved Toby,' said Sam. 'Still do. Always will.'

'Good.'

'I'd never harm him. Not in a real sense… Harm can be a subjective term, ya know.'

'I know it. Nor me. Nor would I ever want to harm a kid like that. I didn't mean… I mean, hell, you saw me!'

'What d'ya mean?'

'Down there.'

'Down there.'

Another silence. And into this silence filtered a certain quiet knowledge.

'Sam.'

Peter Slater

'Wendell.'

Both spoke at once.

More silence, broken again only when each said the other's name again.

Finally, Sam said, 'Am I guessing something right about you?'

'It was for love, Sam. Am I guessing something right about you?'

'It was for love, Wendell. Sehnsucht.'

'Insane sucked, if ya ask me,' Wendell could not resist.

At first, Sam appeared to take this the wrong way. And then he smiled. The two men leant closer to each other; and then, after a small hesitation - which was not doubt but, rather, a relishing of a wonderful moment - kissed.

'We saved a boy's life,' said Sam, when they separated.

'Did I save him from you or did you save him from me?'

'You're so postmodern, Wendell! You're directing the wrong kinda movies.'

'You could help me change track.'

'"Midway through this life…"'

'"… we're bound upon,

I came to myself in a dark wood,

Where the straight way was lost and gone…"' Wendell took up the quote from Dante.

'Hell!' exclaimed Sam. 'You and me… You're the only person I've ever met who could do that kinda thing!'

'We were meant to be, Sammie. Let's get married.'

'D'you think we could last forever?'

'Until the stock of Art, Literature and Music runs out and we've got nothing left to talk about.'

'But there'll still be sex!' said Sam.

They kissed again. Let's leave them now. Some moments are too private even for a book such as this - or perhaps the book you thought this was when you first saw the cover. Let's go out and quietly shut the door behind us.

Chapter Twenty One

Preparations for the wedding - which was to take place at the palace - lasted many months. The work became something of an industry, and the labour expended, if put into monetary terms, might have equalled the GNP of a small Eastern European state. Invitations had to be sent, caterers ordered, new suits and furnishings purchased, musicians hired, transport arranged, and much else besides - as we shall presently see.

And whilst all this was going on, filming had to continue on The Tempest, and daily life at the palace was to be disrupted as little as possible. The guests were still entitled to their perks and adventures.

Sam, restored to his old self, organised everything beautifully. The palace soon got back to its old level of efficiency and service. And if, during filming, Sam - in the part of Caliban - gazed with deep fondness at Toby - in the part of Ariel - well, that was all part of the action and added to the dramatic tension. Film buffs would ponder over those moments for decades to come.

Stills from another movie: Paradise Palace.

Toby sitting naked on a rock, body marked by blue streaks, knees drawn up to his chest: a cheeky sprite.

Wendell, in his Civil War uniform, barking orders through a megaphone.

Sam on the phone in his office.

Sam, seconds after discovering his picture is being taken, one hand raised, mouth open, framing the phrase: 'Get the fuck outa here!'

Russ Schlagfarn dressed in lightweight suit and Panama hat in his wheelchair: he looks mournful.

A group of cheerful naked boys by the pool. One is holding a hose. They are drenched in a shower of water drops.

Sam and Wendell together, in a variety of poses: sharing a strawberry milkshake with a couple of straws in the Paradise restaurant; Sam, in the mud and loincloth of his Caliban costume,

Peter Slater

conferring with the uniformed Wendell on the set of The Tempest; side-by-side on canvas chairs: Wendell reading Light in August by William Faulkner, Sam reading To the Lighthouse by Virginia Woolf; engrossed in a game of chess; on the roof of the palace at sunset, arms around each other's shoulders, gazing out at the desert.

A number of shots of Toby and Jed: sharing a joke on the set of the movie; Toby on his knees before Jed, swallowing the older man's cock almost in its entirety; the two viewed from behind as they walk hand in hand across one of the palace courtyards; a close-up of their faces, heads inclined, just touching.

Sam standing alone, deep in thought; one hand supporting an elbow, the other holding his chin.

'Hey, Toby!' Sam called, one day. 'Come over here, will ya?'

They were in the Paradise Garden, Sam sitting on a grassy bank in the shade of a tree by the lake, Toby passing.

'Hiya, chief!'

'Take a seat here.' Sam patted the ground next to him. If his heart gave a slight tremor, he betrayed no outward sign of excessive emotion. Without being unfriendly, he had avoided any close contact with Toby since the time of the boy's incarceration. 'How ya doin', these days?'

'Good, chief! The movie's comin' along well, ain't it?'

'I'm pleased with it.'

'That Wendell's a good director.'

'He's one of the cinema greats, Toby. When you're an old man you'll be able to say with pride that you once starred in a film directed by Wendell Banks himself.'

'Yeah.'

'You ever think of the future, Toby?'

Toby plucked a long stalk of grass and sucked on it. 'Some,' he said, after a while.

They both gazed at a swan, followed by a troop of grey cygnets, gliding in a V-formation across the lake.

Paradise Palace

'Well, it's a long way off for you,' Sam said.

'No more than for anybody else,' said Toby.

'Eh? Hey, yeah! Suppose you're right. But ya know what I mean. The future's that time when you have less change in your life and when you don't have ta worry about money so much. You can settle down a bit.'

'I don't worry about money so much now. And... And, well, I feel settled.'

'In what way settled?'

'Being here. I'm comfortable here. Happy here. There's a lot of love in this place. It feels good. Deep down. Some places feel just right - as Thoreau said about Walden.'

'You and Jed Howitzer are getting pretty close, aren't ya?' Sam said suddenly.

Toby hesitated before answering with a slow nod, 'Some.' He chewed the blade of grass delicately.

'Some,' echoed Sam.

'Some.'

'I'm an old man, Toby...'

'Oh, not so old, chief,' Toby interrupted.

'I'm an old man,' Sam continued. 'And I've seen a lot of relationships in my time. The momentary, the casual, the semi-permanent, the deep and long-lasting... What I'm trying to say is... From what I've seen, I sense you and Jed are, well, more than close...'

'I'm in love with Jed, chief.' As Toby said these words he felt a warmth around his heart and tears budded in his eyes.

'I think I knew that. I want you to know that I'm so happy.'

'Thanks, chief.'

'Yeah. Toby?

'Yeah, chief?'

'Toby. Call me old-fashioned, but I think marriage is a fine institution.'

'I think so too, chief. And you're never too old.'

'Nor too young. Is Jed in love with you, do ya think? In the same

– 127 –

way that you are with him?'

'I think so.'

'Think so?'

'I know so.'

Sam smiled. 'Toby, I've been talking one or two things over with Wendell, my intended. We've both seen you and Jed together. You're more than a pair, you're a match. We wondered if you'd like to make it a double wedding.' He spoke these last words quickly, briefly glancing at Toby and then away, as if embarrassed at the ultimate awkwardness of his offer.

Toby was silent.

'This never occurred to you, right?' asked Sam.

'Well, no. Of course not, chief.'

'Does the idea strike you as too preposterous?'

Toby shook his head. 'No.'

'So?'

'It's a nice idea…'

'But?'

Toby was silent again a long time. Then, 'Maybe there aren't any "buts". But.'

'But?'

'But, I'd have to ask Jed.'

'You want to marry him?'

'With all my heart.'

'Then you'd better propose!'

'Hey, yeah!' Toby grinned. 'But how the heck does a boy go about doing that? Advise me, chief!'

'No-one knows. It's always a first time. But you could start by going down to the rose garden and finding a single red rose and taking it from there. That's the first step. After that, well, just follow your heart.'

'Follow my heart.'

'It'll lead you right, if you listen carefully enough.'

Toby shook his head in wonderment. Then, abruptly, he stood up. 'Can I go now?'

'Sure! To the rose garden?'

'To the rose garden.'

'Let me know the outcome, soon as possible. There'll be quite some arranging to do.'

'Sure, chief!'

And he was gone.

Sam stared at the water. Somehow, he felt he should have been happy at this juncture. Instead, however, he experienced something like a small collapse of the heart. He stared, until the grey wrinkled surface of the water became a blur.

'Oh, and chief?'

'Wha'?'

Sam looked up. There was Toby back again. His head splintered the sun into a thousand rays.

'What is it, Toby?'

'Chief. I really love you, too. I want you to know that. And, well… you're precious to me.'

'Aw, shucks, Toby!' Sam waved a dismissive hand. 'And I love you.'

'I know it.'

A brightly-coloured flock of parrots flew screeching across the lake, and Sam's recovered heart released him into laughter. Now there were no more clouds hovering over the Paradise Palace: it was clear skies all the way.

On the morning of the wedding, Washington and Curt went early to Toby's room. Tousle-haired and sleepy-eyed, Toby greeted them at the door, wearing a short bathrobe embroidered with pink balloons, triangles, rainbows and the much-repeated slogan, "who's gay now?"

'Time to get ready!' said Washington, his voice sounding hollow in the quietness.

'Aw, gees you guys!' Toby attempted unsuccessfully to stifle a yawn. 'What the heck time is it?'

'Wedding day time!' said Curt. 'Come on.'

They led him back inside, stripped him of his robe and laid him naked on a massage table. Using a combination of cut-throat, safety and electric razors they shaved his body entirely until he was smooth as a new-born piglet. Then they bathed him in delicately-scented water, towelled him down and anointed him with sweet oils and perfumes. When they were done, the combination of scents was so delightful, they were overcome by a strange urge merely to close their eyes and fall asleep beside him, saturated in gorgeous air. But, alas, such was not to be.

The boys set to, making-up Toby's face and manicuring his nails. When this lengthy business was complete, they dressed him.

Toby's wedding suit was made entirely of silver cotton, sewn skilfully to resemble chain mail. It consisted of a sleeveless vest, waistcoat and breeches. He had no undergarments and the sight of his cock, half-hidden and constantly half-erect, was deeply erotic. His shoes were of silver crocodile leather.

'You are perfect!' Curt and Washington exclaimed as one, stepping back to get a proper look at the finished product. A touch here, a dab there, a couple of kisses and the task was complete.

The Paradise Palace was bedecked with flags, bunting and balloons. All that morning, the guests had been arriving by car, coach and helicopter. There were one or two recognisable names on the list: film stars and musicians, a scattering of English Lords and Ladies, a Hungarian Countess; but most of the thousand invitations had gone out to those unknowns who simply had the good fortune of being friends of the betrothed.

The ceremony itself took place, on the stroke of two, in the Great Hall. As the organist launched into a solemn march (accompanied by ethereal, high, held notes from a boy's choir flown over from an English cathedral), the two couples processed up the aisle. Wendell and Sam were dressed in matching white Tuxedos, Jed wore a suit made up of a patchwork quilt of colours and Toby was in his chain mail. Behind

Paradise Palace

them, guided by boys, came a menagerie of creatures: two lambs, shampooed and sporting ribbons and bells, a shaggy-haired, long-horned goat, a crocodile, a baby lion.

The service was conducted by an elderly excommunicated bishop from Ireland (excommunicated by the ironically corrupt established Church, but very much communicated by the Gay Church of Renewal.) The proceedings consisted of a cheerful mix from the Christian, Buddhist, Hindu and Pagan traditions. Vows were promised, (including, in Wendell and Sam's case, a pledge to monogamy), rings exchanged, and each couple had to jump over a magic broomstick.

When all was done, a great cheer went up from the congregation, the choir sang "I Will Survive" and a thousand pink balloons rained down from the rafters.

The banquet was held on the lawns in the Paradise Garden. Beneath canopies, long tables were laden with turkeys, chickens, quail, quail's eggs, fish, salads, a variety of breads, rice, fruit, cakes, ices... There were copious amounts to drink and a Mediaeval band played.

A rottweiler puppy trailed beneath the tables and between the legs of the guests, occasionally stopping for a scrap of fallen food or to allow himself to be petted by a richly manicured hand. The puppy's name was Earl and his collar was fitted with a small microphone and tape recorder. His owner worked for one of the more scurrilous New York daily papers and Earl often picked up useful snippets of society gossip that would otherwise have gone unnoticed. And this is what he heard:

'If there's a nuclear winter, the whole ice-cream market'll collapse worldwide, so I'm selling my shares in Ben and Jerry's and going into lead piping.'

'... a gravity-loss machine. I got some engineers from NASA to install it in the annexe. Forget flotation tanks, you enter a world of zero gravity and all your cares simply slip away. Wouldn't be without it. And I tell you another thing! Bill Clinton is having an affair with...' Sadly, Earl bounded over to feast on a chicken leg just at that critical moment.

'If I could hold one moment forever in eternity it would be that moment when two boys, naked except for tight running shorts, kiss for the first time, and one boy slowly snakes his hand into the waistband of his friend's shorts and touches for the first time that yearning, pulsing cock... He takes the tip between the tips of his fingers and massages gently... The boys' tongues are deep in each other's mouths and the boy being masturbated is groaning helplessly... His friend licks, kisses and gently bites around his neck, his shoulder, his nipples... Then licks his tongue further and further down... He gets to his knees and pulls the shorts down over the other boy's firm, smooth ass. At first he keeps the waistband level with the base of the cock, and nibbles the hard, pulsing shaft, before lowering it beneath the heavy balls. With his friend's shorts now around his thighs, the boy applies himself whole-heartedly to the cock. Nuzzling the length, taking the glans in his mouth. The fellated boy fucks his cock over the other's soft, moist tongue. Pulls out and slaps it against his friend's cheeks, pushes it again into the eager mouth. Now the kneeling boy stands once more and peels his own shorts down. He takes his own cock and the other's in one fist and starts to pump with lustful fury. Both cocks are dripping pre-cum. The only sounds are the boys' groans and the moist frictions of their bodies. They will soon come together for the first time. Their virgin bodies are building to the big climax. Every nerve end is vibrant beneath their skin. They know they must cum at any moment... And then their bodies seem to pause on the edge of a great precipice, before finally tumbling over simultaneously into a great rush of orgasm... When the last shudder has past through them and they are wiping their cum across one another's chests, a sound makes them glance up. There, coming towards them, is the high school basketball coach, their perennial wet dream...'

Earl grabbed the bone and promptly made so much noise slavering over it the next ten minutes of recorded noise were completely obscured. Then, sadly, he encountered the crocodile who, despite being tethered to a stake, still had rope enough to scurry after the tasty puppy dog, bite him in two and swallow him in a couple of greedy gulps. A few of the guests witnessed this vile act - it was all over in a matter of moments and Earl barely had time to squeal, he certainly felt no pain - but none of them were dog lovers, so no alarm was raised and no attention was drawn to the incident. One minute a dog was there, and in the next he was gone: there was no more to it than that. Life can sometimes be cold and cruel.

'This is my third marriage, actually,' Wendell was saying to Mr Springsteen. 'A man in my position needs the security of marital fidelity.'

'What happened to your previous partners?'

'Jim went off with a busboy, Taylor joined a travelling circus and Ben decided he wanted to devote his life to blackmailing Congressmen, and I couldn't abide that sort of career choice, so I left him.'

'I can go along with that.'

'Composed any new songs lately?'

All was going well, it seemed. No guests at any party could possibly have been enjoying themselves more. The food was good, the entertainment unfussy and unobtrusive. Everyone was looking forward to the speeches and the cabaret promised for later that evening.

No-one noticed - how could they have done? - a long trail of cars and vans heading towards the palace in a cloud of red dust.

Trouble was on its way.

Chapter Twenty Two

It was the police.

During his time of madness, Sam had neglected to pay his regular "donation" towards the Sheriff's office, and now here was the result: a posse of twenty cars and half a dozen vans loaded with guns, barking dogs and barking cops.

Sheriff Snopes was a heavy man. Overweight would be an equally accurate description. He lumbered out of the lead car and perspired his way towards the main gate of the palace. He wore a wide brimmed Stetson, dark glasses, a white shirt, cowboy boots with revolving spurs, and chinos. Whilst he rapped the lion's head knocker on the timbered door and called out, 'Open up! It's the Law!', his men surrounded the palace walls.

His knocking and shouting went unheard amidst the merrymaking inside. But Sheriff Snopes had come prepared. Co-ordinating his war-plan through his walkie-talkie, he ordered an immediate and rapid breaching of the palace walls.

Quickly, portable ladders and ropes were produced. The walls were scaled easily. The Paradise Palace did not have any real security system on the outside. There were no rolls of barbed wire, electronic alarms or cameras: Sam believed that high-security was a sign of high-neurosis and he refused to allow it. 'Prepare for war and you get war', he was always quoting Confucius (well, he said it was Confucius, but he was careless at attribution).

Most of the sheriff's men landed in far-forsaken and deserted corners; but he himself, and a faithful band of close followers, found themselves directly in the Paradise Garden, by the lake.

The first guests to see them thought them part of the show.

'Well he-lloo, honey!' greeted a lawyer from Alabama, welcoming Sheriff Snopes by grabbing his crotch and giving it a friendly squeeze. 'Sam hasn't let us down. Uniforms are just my thing and so are men of just a certain age! Are you available?'

Paradise Palace

'I'm a representative of the law here in Arizona, and I aim to see that the law's kept to. You're all under arrest.'

'So true! You've got the manner, the speech, the everything! You're a star, sheriff! A sheriff's star!'

'Where's Sam Greatorix?' Sheriff Snopes asked fiercely.

'Love it! But please arrest me properly first,' begged the lawyer.

'Sure thing!' Sheriff Snopes clapped the man in handcuffs and leg irons and left him leaning joyfully against the wall.

Whilst the lawyer was a simple soul, others were not, and a steady trickle of people began moving away from the newcomers.

The main activity was taking place on the other side of the lake, and the sheriff led his men in that direction.

'Sheriff Wesley Snopes!' Sam spotted the lawman before the lawman had seen him, and marched towards him with a welcoming handshake at the ready. 'Well, how are ya?' Thinking, 'My God! I owe the guy a thousand dollars and I didn't even put him on the guest list! What is wrong with me?', he said aloud: 'Glad you could make it. And you've brought along one or two friends - that's swell!'

A couple of burly deputies eyed a no less burly cohort of film star's bodyguards - all dark glasses and black suits.

'Nothing swell about it, Sam. I've got a warrant issued by Judge Grant in Tucson, calling for your arrest and the closing down of these here premises.'

'Judge Grant, eh? Good fella!' Thinking: 'My God! I owe him two thousand dollars and a visit from a couple of the boys. He should also have got an invite.'

'We have reason to believe that you are illegally running a male brothel...'

'Excuse me, sir,' one of the bodyguards touched the sheriff on the arm and whispered in his ear, 'Would you mind toning down your language in the presence of Miss Taylor?'

'Well, if Miss Taylor hasn't ever in her life heard the words male br... Ah, sorry, Miss Taylor, I didn't see you standing there. It's a pleasure to see you. I've always been a fan. Perhaps later I could have

– 135 –

an autograph for my little girl?'

Miss Taylor smiled, prompting Sheriff Snopes to say, 'Heck, with so much feminine beauty in the world I just don't understand you guys who go chasing around after each other. I mean, I look at my genitals in the mirror every morning and I think ,No, sir! Sorry, Miss Taylor. I meant to say knees. Knees not gen…'

'The world's full of variety, Wesley,' interrupted Sam. 'Perhaps we could go to my office?'

'No, sir. I'm here to arrest you all and I'll do it out here in the open!'

'Wesley,' Sam repeated. 'I think it's imperative you come to my office… I don't think Judge Grant would like it if you didn't come to my office.'

'What's that supposed to mean?'

'Proper procedure.'

Sheriff Snopes made a face.

'What sort of warrant you got there?' asked Sam.

'I got two here. One's for your arrest and the apprehension of anyone caught behaving illegally on these premises; and the other's a search warrant entitling me to enter each and every room on your premises.'

'That's dandy! Come and search my office. Right now. Your men are welcome to eat and drink as much as they like whilst you're gone. Sheriff, you know me and I know you, and you know Judge Grant and I know Judge Grant.'

'A fine upstanding man.'

'Finest man in Arizona! Come to my office a moment, where we can have a quiet discussion.'

Wesley looked about him. He saw, or thought he saw, an array of the rich and famous, including a Secretary of State…

'There are some powerful people here, Wesley. It would be just as well if you followed the proper procedure and made no mistakes.'

'I don't aim to. But…'

'Ten minutes in my office.'

Paradise Palace

Sheriff Snopes took off his hat, bowed towards Miss Taylor, 'I'm obliged to meet you, Ma'am,' and walked away with Sam.

It wasn't just the photographs - although they played their part. Sam Greatorix kept them in a green leather bound volume with HAPPY MEMORIES written on the front in gold letters. Pages one through eight were pasted with pictures of Judge Grant in various poses with various boys. Sitting behind his desk Sam presented them to Wesley in a general way; but he did think particularly to point out the one where Judge Grant was dressed as Little Miss Muffet.

Sheriff Snopes trembled as he leafed through the damning evidence.

'Judge Grant wouldn't like it if these pictures came into the public domain,' said Sam. 'It could make for an uncomfortable time for his Sheriff.'

'But he wants me to arrest you! I gotta do it!'

'He wants me to give him a little phone call. I'll have a few words in his ear. I'll sort everything out. You won't be blamed for anything.' Sam nodded confidentially. 'And how're your children? You still managing to afford to put them through private school?'

'Well, you know...' Wesley shifted awkwardly and rubbed his finger beneath his shirt collar. 'It's hard on a sheriff's wages.'

'I haven't forgotten you,' said Sam. 'Perhaps we can get back to our usual arrangement? I'm sorry if I might have seemed to have lapsed in the past few weeks. I've been unwell.'

'Oh, now, hey, I...' Sheriff Snopes held his hand over the desk in a conciliatory gesture. 'I don't mean, I...'

'A small glass of bourbon, Wesley?' Sam produced a bottle and two glasses, which already contained ice.

Wesley scratched his cheek, 'That's mighty kind of you, Sam, but...'

'Good!' Sam poured the drinks. 'Cheers, Wesley!' He lifted his drink and waited until Wesley did the same and they chinked glasses. 'A deal.'

Peter Slater

Wesley took a sip, then put down his glass. 'I'm not sure, Sam. Ya know, I… What about my men? I've got a hundred men out there, how am I going to explain to them that we just turn back without any arrests.'

'All men are human, Wesley. Ya wanna know somethin'? Then come over here and take a look at some sights.'

He led the sheriff over to another desk on which stood a large video screen sectioned into a dozen parts.

'Our closed circuit TV system. We like to record all the sex that goes on here. I sell the videos to China - now that is a secret between you and me. Look here. What do ya see in that top left hand corner, there? And there on the right. And in the centre. And there. And there. And… if I just give a couple, of clicks here to change the pictures… 'Ah, yes!'

Sheriff Wesley Snopes gazed in astonishment.

'Is this now?' he asked.

'Live TV!'

The pictures were all of his men making love to the boys at the palace.

'And there's more, I'll wager,' said Sam. 'I expected as much. Your guys don't waste time when they visit.'

'But…'

'But, Wesley. I know something you don't. You are the only straight law officer in the entire county. You're the only man I know of who has never visited my palace for… personal reasons.'

There might have been some exaggeration in this statement, but it hardly mattered. Sam had made his point.

'Let's go back and join the celebration, Wesley,' said Sam. 'It's my wedding day, ya know.'

'Ya don't say?'

'Sure. Come on. There's good food and drink and you can have a little chat with Miss Taylor - that should impress your wife. How is Laura-Lee, by the way?'

'Aw, she's fine. Sends her love.'

'She knew you were coming along here?'
'Can't keep nothin' from ol' Laura-Lee!'
Sam clapped the sheriff on the back and the two men went to rejoin the party.

A condor flew high over the palace and this is what he saw: knots of people chatting and laughing, a film star doing an impersonation of Bill Clinton, lawmen and boys making love, the trees, the lawns, the sheep and cows, the lake. And an old man in a wheelchair. The man is Russ Schlagfarn. He is alone. A tartan shawl covers his lap. On his face is a smile of absolute bliss. The sight of burly uniformed men always did do a special something for him. The condor, scenting prey, circled. It recognised the man as dead. Should it swoop down to pluck out the man's eyes?

Oh, no way! Will you get outa here! Go on and do something else! Pluck out the man's eyes! I mean ta say! There's no more in this book. That condor, he just had a look and flew back to his eyrie high in the mountains.
And that's it.